WAR'S PASSION

DRAGONS OF ARES, BOOK ONE

LIA DAVIS

War's Passion

Dragons of Ares, Book 1

© copyright 2014-2019 Lia Davis

Published by Davis Raynes Publishing Group, LLC

PO Box 224

Middleburg, FL. 32050

Cover Art by Jacqueline Sweet

Formatting by Glowing Moon Designs

For those who share my love for dragons.

War's Passion

After losing her parents in a brutal attack from a monster straight out of her nightmares, Gwendolyn Preston tries to pick up the shattered pieces of her life. Along with her best friend, she moves to a small fishing village on the coast of Maine to find a new life away from the nightmares that haunt her. Just when she believes her life could go back to normal, the deliciously dark and handsome Markus Sullivan disrupts her hopes to grieve in peace.

Markus drew the short straw when it came to being the liaison between his father, Ares—God of War—and his brothers. When he discovers that the earth bound demi-gods, known as the descendants, have banded together to start another rebellion against the gods, it becomes his number one priority to stop them.

That is until he meets Gwen, the granddaughter of Aphrodite, and the next target of the descendants. Together, their path is rife with passion and danger. It might take more than the son of War to win this battle... Gwen herself.

CHAPTER ONE

A cold sensation rolled down Gwen's spine like an icy finger as she stepped out onto the back porch of her parents' Florida home. She focused her senses out into the cool evening, and inhaled the fragrance of night jasmine lingering on the breeze. The moonless, star-filled sky didn't chase away the feeling of menace lurking in the shadows, waiting. The awareness had clung to her since she'd woken that morning and she wished she could feel the creatures of the night like her best friend and adopted sister, Elle, could. Although Gwen descended from the gods themselves, sensing monsters wasn't her gift. As the great-granddaughter of Nyx, goddess of the night, Elle could see into the dark-ness and all her secrets.

Descended from the goddess of love, Gwen held the power of persuasion, and she could sway people, espe-cially men, to bend to her will. The gift came from her father's side of the family—Tom Preston was one of Aphrodite's earthborn sons.

She loved nights like this as well as the calm that blanketed the small town of Perry. It was a few minutes before midnight and everyone slept. Elle had left early that morning to show her latest paintings and sculptures at a gallery in Jacksonville. It was the first time the girls had been apart since becoming friends in the third grade.

The sound of glass breaking behind her made Gwen's heart hammer and her stomach clench. Spinning, she saw three large men charge into her home through what used to be the front door. Splintered wood lay half in the kitchen, half in the living room, and the long rectangular windows on either side of the entrance were destroyed. Glass littered the living room floor.

Fear rushed through her like wildfire and she darted to the side to hide behind the curtain of the sliding glass door. Helplessness consumed her as she watched one of the men open drawers to her father's desk, dumping the contents on the floor. Another searched the living room, then stepped into the kitchen. Her heart sank as the third man turned toward the hallway.

Mom, Dad.

Without another thought for her own safety, she rushed after the man that went down the hall. Before she could make it, another man crashed into her, slamming her to the ground. Sharp, stabbing pain shot from her hip down her leg. Gwen screamed, hoping to wake her parents, as she clawed at the man's face, aiming for his eyes.

A loud thump followed by her mother's cry reached Gwen's ears. Terror filled her, cold and crippling. Tears ran down her cheeks. A moment later the man that went towards her parents' room flew backwards through the living room, and further until he crashed into the kitchen island. Then her father stood at the hallway entrance, hands fisted by his side.

"Let her go."

Gwen stared at her father in disbelief. His body glowed with power.

"You think to use mortal magic on me?" The man holding her laughed, then released Gwen and rose to his feet.

A bright flash of black and gold light filled the room, leaving a large black dragon where the man had been. Disbelief and horror twined through her veins as she stared at the creature. Smoke rolled out its long snout and the eyes almost glowed red. Shaking, she managed to scramble backwards to keep from being trampled by the beast—which was way too big for the house.

Her father held his hands out from his body, palms facing the dragon. A soft white light beamed from the center of his hands, then brightened and grew into a ball of bright white energy the size of cantaloupe before her father thrust it at the dragon.

Gwen screamed again, not knowing what she could

do. There was a freaking dragon inside her home and her father…well, she didn't know what he threw at the beast because he'd never used his magic to that extent before. The ball of light didn't do anything but drive the dragon back a step. The beast whipped his tail around to hit Gwen. The blow knocked her out the back door. Landing on the deck, she watched in horror as the dragon breathed fire toward her father.

Tears streaming down her face, she shouted for her father to get out, but too late. Flames covered him and he stumbled forward, igniting the carpet with each step and the couch as he fell. The dragon let out a roar that rocked the house. The men that came with him rushed outside right before the beast blew out another blast of fire and swiveled his head around the room. The whole house engulfed in flames within seconds.

Agony ripped through Gwen's heart and she sobbed, but no one heard her.

CHAPTER TWO

F ourteen years later

"Don't you just love it?"

Stepping out of her Audi, Gwen seriously doubted her best friend's ability to see. "Elle, it's a lighthouse. An old lighthouse that looks like it should be condemned."

Gwen studied the house, trying her best to look on the positive side. Built onto the original tower of the lighthouse was a three-story old Victorian-style home. Faded wood siding revealed cracked and weathered paint. The roof lacked shingles in several spots.

That was what she got for letting Elle make the final decision about where they lived. Gwen had picked the coast of Maine for the sheer beauty of the cliffs, rocky shores, and beautiful lighthouses. Not to mention the ocean.

So Elle had picked the house. Gwen should have known it'd be a fixer-upper. Elle was an artist, after all.

Her best friend looped her arm with Gwen's and squeezed. "It has so much potential. I know you can't see it now, but trust me, hon. I'll make it a masterpiece. The realtor gave me the number of a great and reasonably priced local contractor."

Letting out a soft sigh, Gwen returned Elle's affection by wrapping an arm around her shoulders. Trust had never been an issue between them. They'd known each other since the third grade and lived together since high school. Elle's parents died in a plane crash when Elle was sixteen and Gwen's parents had taken her in. The two of them hadn't been apart since.

With bottom lip stuck out and eyes wide, Elle faced her and blinked, once. Gwen hated when she made the lost puppy face. It was nearly impossible to turn down. With her straight black hair hanging loose around her shoulders under the oversize brimmed straw hat she wore to keep the sun off her face, Elle batted her lashes. "It'll be fun. The two of us starting over. We can redesign the whole house."

Gwen smiled, unable to say no. Plus, it did sound like a fun project to work on together. It would definitely give her mind something to do and could help keep the demons at bay. "Okay. Let's go inside and see what the damage is."

Elle squealed and clapped as she whirled around to

jog up the steps. The porch with its missing slats and aged wood looked like it would cave any moment.

Well, that was the first thing they'd have to fix before someone broke a leg.

"Be careful." Gwen followed her friend into the house and almost gagged. She cupped her mouth and nose. "It smells like someone died in here."

Elle crinkled up her nose. "It didn't smell like this last month when I came to see it."

"Well, something must've crawled in here and decided to make the house its final resting place." Gwen rushed to the closest window and opened it.

Without responding, Elle hurried around and opened the rest of the windows in the living room.

The inside looked better than the outside, which wasn't saying too much. The open floor plan spread out before Gwen. Large windows on either side of her illuminated the interior. *Okay, so maybe it does have potential. As long as we can get rid of that awful smell.*

To her left, a spiral staircase crawled from the back corner of the room and vanished into the ceiling. A smile lifted her lips and she drifted over and tested the bottom step, then placed a hand on the railing and gave a little shake. It appeared sturdy.

"Go on up. The realtor had the stairs replaced to show off the place." Elle came up behind her.

"Hmm. That was nice of them," Gwen said dryly and continued up the stairs.

On the top floor, Gwen glanced around in awe. The

space appeared to be in better shape than downstairs, except for the cobwebs and mounds of dust everywhere.

Elle leaned into her. "You like it, don't you?"

Gwen rolled her eyes for effect, but couldn't hide her pleasure. "I have to admit, it does have character."

Smile widening, Elle turned to the right. "I've already picked the rooms. Come on." Gwen followed her into one of the large bedrooms. "This one is yours because it has a great view of the ocean."

Warmth and happiness filled Gwen's heart. Her sister knew Gwen's love of the ocean well. Being able to open the windows on summer nights and listen to the waves crash against the rocks would be heaven.

Elle turned to face her with a gleam in her eyes that rivaled a child's on Christmas morning. "So...can we keep it?"

A laughed bubbled out of Gwen. "Yes. You have your project house to work your magic on."

The next instant, Elle leaped toward her and hugged her tight. "This is going to be so much fun. Our own place and a fresh start."

Gwen agreed. Yep, a fresh start, away from the nightmares of fire-breathing dragons chasing her.

Markus sat at his dark cherry-stained oak desk in the large estate he shared with his brothers, Drake, Ty, Seth, and Zavier. The mansion sat high on the coastal Maine cliff, overlooking a small fishing village named Serenity Cove.

Many of the locals called the large house a castle, which in a way it was. Ty and Seth designed the structure and the five of them had built it—about five hundred years before, after they were cast from the Heavens thanks to Garrick's betrayal.

Fisting his hand over the keyboard of his laptop, he ground his teeth. The mere thought of Garrick made Markus's blood boil. The male wanted vengeance against him and his brothers as well as the gods. Markus believed the motive for his brother's rage against them steamed from the death of his mate.

After leaning back in his black leather chair, Markus studied his brothers. Drake sat across from his desk with a tablet in his hand and a notebook balanced on one knee, his dark brows drawn together as he read something on the computer screen. He scrubbed a hand over his shaved head and lifted his brown gaze to Markus's.

The male's dragon flashed in his eyes, but Markus ignored it. Drake submitted to his animal half more than the rest of them. He was just as aggressive and deadly in human form as he was as a dragon so he avoided crowds and almost never went into the village without one of his brothers—usually Markus or Ty to play escort.

Drake was content to stay home and research news feeds, tabloid sites, and magazines for reports of "the strange and unusual." He gathered information about magical beings, angels, dragon attacks, or anything suspicious in order to find some clue to the whereabouts of Garrick.

To Markus's right, Zavier sat at the small round table. His light brown hair fell into his eyes as he worked on the household's monthly finances. If it had anything to do with a computer, security, or money, it was Zavier's domain.

Quiet and reserved was the best way to describe Z. His love for technology and being left alone made him their best resource. There wasn't a software program in existence that he couldn't hack.

Behind Z, in the far corner of the room, Seth held his cell phone pressed to his ear. With his supernatural hearing, Markus could tell it was a business call. Seth was the co-owner of Sullivan Contractors.

Ty was the other owner.

Seth was the playful one. He always had a smartass remark or a prank up his sleeve. Even his dragon liked to play with its prey before killing it. His high level of energy and aggression needed to be released regularly or he made Drake seem like a big pussycat.

Moving his gaze from Seth, Markus met Ty's stare and arched a brow. "Do you have anything to report?"

Ty's mouth twitched, which did nothing to reveal the other dragon's mood, especially with the damned sunglasses he wore all the time. Markus understood the reason behind the shades. The upper right-half of his face was scarred and left his eye unable to shift back to a human appearance. An injury he received when

Garrick and his Imperials had held him captive. Something Ty never spoke of it.

"I have nothing." Ty turned his gaze to Scth in interest.

Markus turned to Drake. "Anything on your end?"

"Nada. It's like the bastard fell off the earth or something."

A growl rose from Markus's chest. "We should be so lucky. The coward is hiding. I want him flushed out. What was his last known activity?"

"A small town in Nebraska a few weeks ago." Drake scrolled though his electronic notes.

"Why a small town?" Markus sat up in his seat.

Shaking his head, Drake sat back in his chair. "Don't know. All I've been able to gather are sightings of a winged man walking out of a cornfield. The article is filled with a bunch of stuff about the witness being an older man and that it was dark when he saw it and so on. I did find out there was a police report filed by a woman named Gwendolyn Preston a few days before the old man's sighting. Her complaint says she was being stalked."

Markus drew his brows tighter. "Do you think the two events are connected?"

"I'm suspicious of everything strange. I had Zavier hack into the police records and guess what?" Drake shrugged.

"The police didn't find anything."

"That or they didn't care to look. There was some

bullshit about how no strangers came to town and Ms. Preston was being paranoid." Drake growled before continuing. "I also had Z looking into the woman's medical history. She was treated at a psychiatric hospital for about six months after her parents were attacked in their home and killed."

Markus raised a brow for Drake to continue, but Zavier spoke next. "I believe her parents were attacked by a dragon."

"Fuck," Ty and Markus said at the same time. Markus ran a hand through his hair and said, "How long ago?"

"Fourteen years. The house burned down and both bodies were charred beyond recognition. I hacked into the medical examiner's personal files and found notes about gouges on the female's bones. The ME placed time of death before the fire started. It's possible she was mauled to death. The husband didn't have any other cause of death besides thermal injuries—he was burned alive."

"Seeing your parents killed by a mythical creature would be reason enough to see a shrink." Ty sat forward in his chair and shook his head.

Shoving his phone into his pocket, Seth crossed the room and joined the conversation. "So we're mythical creatures now, are we?"

A smile tugged at Ty's mouth. "Straight out of humans' nightmares."

Seth shrugged. "I have proof that we're the object of some of their fantasies."

"Yeah, in your fantasies." Ty snorted.

After a brief grin, Seth turned serious. "I just got off the phone with a new resident to Serenity Cove. Her name is Danielle Roberts and she and her sister just bought the old lighthouse down the beach."

"What are you not saying? It's not like you to bring contracting business to all of our attention." Markus asked.

"Her sister's name is Gwen Preston." Seth nodded.

Drake, Zavier, and Ty all cursed at the same time and Markus stared at Seth for a brief moment in disbelief. *Could it really be so easy?*

"Ty, I want you and Seth to meet with the women in the morning. See if this Gwen is a descendent." Markus sat back in his chair. "Zavier, email me the files on the woman."

Zavier nodded and typed on his keyboard. A few seconds later Markus's phone beeped, indicating he had a new message. Turning to his computer, he logged into his email account. Too many unanswered questions revolved around this Gwen Preston. He wanted to know more about her, but mostly he wanted to know why Garrick attacked her parents.

CHAPTER THREE

A knock sounded on the door and Gwen froze as she stepped off the spiral staircase. Frowning, she crossed the room and peeked through the peephole. Two large men stood on the other side. Panic flooded her and her heart pounded. Closing her eyes, she tried to breathe.

Calm down. You're spooking yourself again.

"Who is it?" she asked, not that it would help if they were murderers. Seriously, she needed to get over the nightmares.

"We're with Sullivan Contracting. You called us yesterday."

Gwen let out a sigh and plastered a smile on her face. When she opened the door, however, she had to bite her lower lip to keep the gasp from escaping. They weren't just huge, they were gorgeous. Both had short black hair and well-sculpted and muscular bodies, but one was at least four inches taller than the other. The taller one wore a pair of sunglasses even though it was an overcast, dreary day.

"Aphrodite." The shorter man breathed, drawing her attention to him.

"Excuse me?"

He smiled slowly, an expression so devastatingly loaded with charm, she was sure it proved a potent weapon against women everywhere. "Has anyone ever told you that you are as beautiful as Aphrodite?"

Gwen turned her head and stepped aside to allow them entry. Her cheeks warmed while her heart broke a little. Her father told her all the time how much she looked like her grandmother, but she wasn't about to tell a stranger that. "I'm afraid not. My sister went to the store to get a few things. She should be back soon."

The shorter man, who wasn't short at all since he towered over her five foot five height, held his hand out. "Sorry to be rude. I'm Seth Sullivan and this is one of my brothers, Ty."

Gwen shook his hand, and then offered hers to Ty. Instead of taking it, he grunted and gave her a nod before he left them alone to inspect the living room. She glanced at Seth. "Should I be offended?"

She swore she heard Seth growl before moving his gaze to hers. "Don't be. He was born an ass. You mentioned your sister earlier. Would that be Danielle Roberts?"

Gwen nodded. "Yes. Actually, she's my adopted

sister. My parents took her in when we were in high school."

"You mind if we just look around? This place has been vacant for a long time with no caretakers. I have a few safety concerns I want to check out." His interest in safety first resonated with Gwen.

"Sure. Elle's an artist and loves a good project." Maybe she overshared, but she didn't want them to think that she and Elle weren't aware of the home's issues.

Seth raised a brow. "Elle?"

"Oh, Danielle. Our family calls her Elle."

"Ah. Makes sense. Ty is short for Tyson."

At Seth's explanation, Ty growled. Apprehension shivered up Gwen's spine. The growl sounded too close to the one haunting her nightmares.

She had to force her feet in place and shove her hands in her pocket before the man noticed her shaking. Gods, she was such a baby. Years of therapy and she still wasn't over the fear of dragons jumping out of the walls.

As if he sensed her mood shift, Ty turned his head toward her and pressed his lips into a hard thin line. "I'm going to check the upstairs."

Seth touched her arm and she jumped. "Hey, you okay?"

Nodding, she forced a smile and met his gaze. "Yes. It's just…never mind. It's nothing."

The tension in her muscles eased when he didn't

press her for the answers she wouldn't give a stranger. Hell, she had a hard time telling Elle at first and the two of them had their own special…gifts. She motioned him to the kitchen. "You said Ty was one of your brothers. How many do you have?"

Seth laughed. "Four, counting Ty. We live in the large house just south of here."

Gwen stopped and studied him. "You mean the castle on the cliff?"

"Yep. Although it's not really a castle. Too small. Where are you from?"

Too small for a castle? What exactly did he think was 'big'?

Her stomach tightened at his question, but she tamped it down. He was just trying to be friendly. "Florida originally, but we moved to Nebraska about fourteen years ago."

In the kitchen, he opened one of the windows and inspected the frame. "What made you decide to come to Maine?"

Nerves fluttering, she rolled the outer seam to her jeans between her thumb and index finger. *Where the hell was Elle?* "I don't know, really. I love the ocean and the coast of Maine looked beautiful in pictures." A soft laughed escaped her. It probably seemed a little odd to just move to an unknown place based on Internet photos. However, she couldn't tell him she was running from a monster.

If he noticed anything amiss in her behavior, Seth didn't comment. "So what do you think so far?"

"It's more beautiful in person." And it really was.

Seth nodded and walked out of the kitchen in quick, long strides. Gwen had to almost jog to catch up with him. When she reached the living room, the front door opened and Elle came in with her arms full of bags. Gwen rushed over to take a few, but Seth beat her to it and took all the bags. Meeting her sister's gaze and holding in a smile at Elle's raised brows, she could tell by Elle's expression they were thinking the same thing. *Big, strong, and handsome. Hello, Maine.*

"Oh, thanks." Elle took off her large floppy hat and studied Seth for a long moment before she extended her hand. "I'm Elle."

Seth smiled and gave a short nod. "I'm Seth. We spoke on the phone last night."

At her sister's forced smile, real fear froze Gwen's blood. A shadow passed over Elle and her dark brown eyes shimmered slightly. Something was wrong. "Elle?"

Shifting her gaze to Gwen, Elle relaxed and shook her head. "It's fine. I'm fine. The sun peeked through the clouds a couple of times and I feel a little off, but I'm fine." Shifting her gaze back to Seth, she motioned to the kitchen. "You can set the bags down in here."

No you're not. However, Gwen wasn't going to cause a scene in front of their new neighbors and contractors so she kept quiet and followed them to the kitchen. She'd just have to wait until they left to freak out on her sister.

No need to make *everyone* believe she was crazy.

Ty, get your ass down here. There are two of them. Nyx, goddess of night, just walked through the door. Seth sent the telepathic comment to his brother as he and the females walked back into the living room.

Unbelievable. Generally, descendants didn't group together unless they knew their relations. However, by the low dose of magic Seth could sense, he guessed the women's powers had been bound. Yet, they still carried enough of their godly energy that he could tell to which goddess they had been born.

"So, have you looked around? What do you think?" Elle's voice brought his thoughts back to the subject at hand.

"The place isn't too bad. It is definitely restorable. You said last night that you don't want to change anything structural, right?" Seth sensed his brother before Ty came to stand next to him.

"That's right. Gwen and I decided to keep the same layout and add some modern touches." Elle shifted her gaze to Ty. The silver in her pale green eyes shimmered and she pursed her lips before turning to Gwen. "I got the bathroom cleaner you asked for, along with shampoo and soap."

Gwen smiled as if thankful for the distraction. "Oh good. If you will excuse me?"

As soon as Gwen was out of earshot, Elle leaned in and spoke through her teeth. "Dragons."

Inching closer to her, Ty growled, "How long have you had your sight?"

Straightening, Elle folded her arms and stared at them as if debating her next move. "As long as I can remember."

Seth chuckled. "We know what happened to Gwen's parents, or at least we have our theories."

Glancing once in the direction her sister had gone, Elle put the oversized hat back on and pulled down her sleeves to cover her hands. "Come on, I'll show you the outside."

Seth glanced at Ty, who shrugged, and they followed her to the side yard overlooking the ocean. Elle spoke without turning to face them. "We know that we are descendants of the gods. Gwen is the granddaughter of Aphrodite and I'm, like, the great-granddaughter of Nyx. Gwen stopped believing after her parent were killed."

"Why?" Seth frowned.

She dropped her shoulders. "Gwen said she didn't want to believe in any goddess who would let her own son die."

Witnessing her parents' murder had undoubtedly left its mark on Gwen, but even gods were bound by rules.

"The gods are forbidden to have any type of connection with their earth-bound offspring. Aphrodite didn't have a choice. You both have to understand that."

Elle tugged the hat down further on her face and he wondered if the small amount of sunlight peeking through the clouds bothered her. Being a descendant of night had some disadvantages, like being allergic to the sun's rays. "I know that. I tried to tell her the gods can't interfere with human will. Although her parents being slaughtered by a dragon isn't really human will, is it?"

No, it wasn't and that pissed him off. Still, Aphrodite couldn't make *direct* contact. Of course, if she interfered indirectly—such as saving the life of her granddaughter, they still wouldn't have been aware of the goddess's actions.

"Did she really see who did it?" Ty asked before Seth could get the words out.

Elle nodded. "She said it was a black dragon."

"Fuck," Seth breathed. "Why would he kill them?"

Elle whirled on them, her green eyes darker now with silver ringing the pupil. "You know who did it?"

Seth ignored her question, his attention on Ty. "And why would he not take Gwen?"

A knowing grin spread on his face. "He couldn't see her."

Elle waved a hand between them. "Hello? Who didn't see who?"

Ty gazed down at Elle. "Be at the estate at seven

tonight and bring Gwen." Stepping back several feet, he shifted into his red and gold dragon and took flight.

Seth sighed. "He's such a show off. Please don't be late." He ran toward the edge, jumped, and shifted in midair. The women didn't need contractors—they needed protection.

CHAPTER FOUR

M arkus closed his eyes as he stroked his fingers over the keys of the baby grand piano in the great room. The music flowed and filled the air around him, and twined in his soul. He loved the peace it offered. Each note calmed his inner beast in a way nothing else did.

A shift of energy made him opened his eyes. Releasing a low annoyed groan, he stared into Aphrodite's sky blue gaze. She wore a white pants suit and her blond hair hung in thick waves around her shoulders. He stopped playing and slammed the cover over the keys.

The goddess straightened from where she leaned over the side of the piano and folded her arms. "Why did you stop? You know I love to hear you play."

Standing, he gave her his back and peered out the

French doors leading to the gardens in the backyard. "What do you want, Aphrodite?"

Glancing over his shoulder, he saw her roll her eyes, sit down on the bench, and cross her legs. With a little sigh, she opened the cover over the keys and smiled at him. "Nothing," she sing-songed. "I'd thought I would stop by and visit with one of my favorite dragons."

Markus snorted—the goddess never just stopped by. She always had a purpose for her visits. It usually meant he would have to be involved in something dangerous, annoying, or odd. "Have you seen War?"

One slender shoulder raised in a shrug and she pressed the C key. "No. I think he's avoiding me."

"That makes two of us." Markus studied her for several moments. She seemed preoccupied. Usually she hovered close to him or his brothers when she wanted something and annoyed them in a motherly way in her effort to bend them to her will. Yet, tonight she just ran a finger back and forth over the keys, not making a sound. "What's wrong?"

Not looking at him, she sighed. "Gwendolyn needs your help."

Dread hit him in the gut, then crept its way up his spine. If Aphrodite was asking him for help, it couldn't be good. Usually the gods didn't give three shits about the demi-gods. "Why me?"

A sad smile formed on her face as she held his gaze. "Because I can't get involved any more than I already am. Her life is in danger. Besides, she's the last of my mortal children."

Blowing out a breath, he ran a hand through his hair. "I don't know what I can do." That was a lie. No matter how much he told himself that, he knew what he had to do. Garrick couldn't be allowed to unlock any more descendants' powers. The balance of the worlds was shifting.

Aphrodite stood and narrowed her gaze. "Yes, you do. Protect her. Keep Garrick from capturing her." Then she dematerialized and ended the argument. Playing bodyguard—especially to the goddess of love's granddaughter—was the last thing he wanted.

The front door opened and Markus whirled around to find Ty and Seth stalking toward him with purpose in their steps. Ty curled his lip and growled. "I smell Aphrodite."

"She just left." Markus bet their arrival was why she chose to leave. Like so many others, the goddess wasn't comfortable around Ty. Markus didn't blame her, really. Ty was different since his captivity and release. No longer Seth's partner in crime when it came to pranks and parties with the females. After he escaped the Imperials' prison, something in him broke. It was like the bastards extracted the fun-loving, compassionate male he'd once been right out of him and darkened his soul.

Aphrodite once told Markus she feared Ty would turn rogue. So she stayed clear from him when she visited.

Seth stepped around their brother, headed to the mini-bar in the corner of the room, and opened the small refrigerator. After pulling out a beer, he gestured to them in a silent question if they wanted one. "Both women are descendants."

Giving his brother a short nod, Markus paced to the bar and sat. Seth grabbed a beer and handed it to him. The day kept getting better. Descendants never hung out together. It was part of the curse that bound their powers, but now he wasn't so sure. "Gwen is Aphrodite's granddaughter. Who is the other female related to?"

"Nyx. Why was the goddess of love here?" Seth frowned.

Markus stilled, the beer bottle inches from his lips. The goddess of night didn't have many descendants. In fact, she was a personification of night and couldn't take human form for long periods of time. So, as far as he understood, she'd never bothered with humans.

Meeting Seth's gaze, he asked, "Are you sure she's Nyx's?"

Seth nodded and downed his beer. "Yep, she could see our dragons."

Damn. He filed the knowledge, along with his questions, away for later. Right now, they needed to figure out a way to keep the women off Garrick's radar.

"Aphrodite wants me to guard her granddaughter," Markus said dryly.

Ty shook his head with a grin plastered on his face. "Better you than me. I will warn you, she's skittish."

Seth waved his beer in Ty's direction as if dismissing him. "She is not. A little timid, maybe."

"Great." Markus groaned and scrubbed a hand over his face.

"Seth, tell him the best part."

"They're coming to dinner tonight." Seth rolled his eyes.

Markus jerked his head in Seth's direction. "You invited them here? What the hell were you thinking?"

Seth sighed as if bored, which only pissed Markus off more. "Gwen doesn't have faith in Aphrodite anymore. Her 'sister' said it stems from the attack on her parents. So I figured we'd bring them here so that you could explain things so Gwen wouldn't freak out and run."

A burst of laughter almost made Ty fall off his barstool. Markus ignored him and fixed a hard stare on Seth, not missing the fact that Seth said Markus could explain to the female. Why in Hades did everyone think he'd be better suited to handle the woman? "What makes you think she'll listen to me?

"Because you're the leader. Everyone listens to the one in charge." Seth shrugged.

Markus took a step forward then stopped as something dawned on him. Aphrodite's concern for the female was too real. Not that it shouldn't be, but the gods never showed their feelings to them or anyone else. It was a sign of weakness. Yet the goddess came to him and, even as she told him to watch over Gwen, she held a plea in her eyes.

"Aphrodite said Garrick is looking for her."

Seth nodded. "We gathered that. I also think that Aphrodite shielded Gwen during the attack."

"How so?"

"It's just a hunch, but why else would Garrick kill her parents and not take Gwen with him?" Seth had a point.

"That makes sense. She could shield Gwen from his sight and not come into direct contact with her."

"That's why I told Elle to bring Gwen over for dinner tonight. We need to show her she can trust us. Trust that we aren't the monster Gary is." Seth smirked once, certainty ringing in his words.

Markus shook his head at the nickname Seth had given Garrick after their banishment. "Very well. I'll go tell the nymphs that we'll be having guests."

GARRICK PACED the open space of his living quarters inside the command center of Imperial Order—the organization he'd created to bring down the Sons of War and the gods. He grew more impatient with each day and minute that passed. The idiot Imperial in charge of capturing Gwen and bringing her to him had failed, *again*.

Now the bitch had packed up and left town. To make matters worse, she'd burned down the house she'd lived in—successfully preventing him from using a locator spell. "Damn it!"

"He was weak."

Garrick jerked his gaze to the female lounging on his sofa. Ashlynn, or Ash as she liked to be called, was one of the few female descendants he had working for him and one of his best hunters. That didn't surprise him, considering she was related to Artemis, goddess of the hunt.

"Apparently," he growled. "That female is a second generation, like you, and will be very useful to me when her powers are unlocked."

Not only would her power of persuasion be beneficial, so would her ability to make men lust after her like crazed animals. That kind of power was just what he needed to start another war between mankind and the gods.

This time the descendants would prevail and Garrick would rule both worlds.

Ash prowled like a cat toward him. A sensual smile curved her full lips and she ran a finger down his chest to the top of his jeans before leaning close. "I'll find the female for you."

Before he'd told her no, that he wanted her close to base. Now, he was out of options. "Very well, Ash. You can go." Looping an arm around her waist, he jerked her forward so her breasts pressed against him. It was too bad their clothes were in the way. "Be warned, love. Do not betray me."

She took his bottom lip between her teeth and sucked before releasing it then stepped out of his embrace. "Why would I do that?"

Garrick growled low as he watched her sway out of his quarters. *Why, indeed?*

All females betrayed their lovers sooner or later.

CHAPTER FIVE

G wen fidgeted with the hem of her blouse while she waited with Elle in the stone entry of her new neighbors' home—the five men lived in a large castle-like mansion on a high cliff over the Atlantic Ocean. The mansion towered over her, dominating the landscape as she emerged from the car moments ago, but being this close to it gave her chills and made her stomach roll into knots. Scanning the stone facing around her, she spied a gargoyle perched in one of the corners a few feet to the right of the large wood double door. After staring at the thing, she wondered if it was real or just a statue.

The gray stone exterior reminded her of something out of a horror movie, or at least a paranormal thriller. *Perfect place to dump the bodies.*

Elle covered her hand, drawing Gwen's attention to her best friend. "It'll be fine. You can trust them."

"How do you know?"

"I know." Elle tapped her temple and winked. "Now, stop worrying."

Gwen knew she could trust Elle's judgment—she could sense darkness in people and see the creatures that humans believed to be fables.

The door opened to an elderly looking man in a tuxedo. Yet, the man didn't seem like he was fully human. She wasn't sure what he was, but his magical signature flowed around him in slow iridescent waves. His aura was warm, soft, and welcoming. It was nothing like she'd ever sensed before. Gwen leaned into Elle and said through her teeth, "They have a butler."

Smiling, Elle whispered, "Shut it and smile."

A giggle threatened to bubble out. *Oh, great. Here comes the hysterics, and in front of strangers.* Anxiety always rose when she met new people.

The butler gave them a short bow. "Good evening."

Gwen nodded, but didn't pay too much attention as she entered the foyer. The house was even bigger on the inside. Massive staircases were on either side of her, and straight ahead was a large great room. The room was decorated in Grecian art and accented by red and gold drapes that reached from ceiling to floor.

Elle looped her arm with Gwen's and together they walked into the great room where five men sprawled in various activities. The two she recognized, Seth and Ty, sat on the sofa playing a video game. Two more perched on barstools next to a mini-bar on the far end of the room. With his hands stuffed in his pockets, the fifth man peered out a window away from the others.

Studying the man at the window, Gwen felt a strange pull toward him that she'd never experienced before. The feeling was more of a knowing. There was something familiar about him—which was ridiculous, because she'd never met him before. As if sensing her intense stare, he turned. Gwen took a step back at the intensity in his gaze—his eyes were so dark, they looked black.

When he walked toward her, her heart sped up and a wave of hot desire rushed through her. Without realizing it, she crossed the room until they met in the middle. She blinked as he raised his hand and ran his knuckles down her cheek.

"Impossible." He whispered, but it didn't quite register.

Breaking eye contact, he took her hand and spoke with a smooth, but husky voice. "I'm Markus."

"Hi." Wow. Was that all she had? A gorgeous man touched her and suddenly she regressed to fifteen, crushing on the quarterback? *You're pathetic.*

Gathering what composure she had left, she tugged her hand out of his and stepped away. She needed to clear her head. "This is a beautiful house."

"Thank you."

His husky, sensual reply heated her skin, making it feel tight and highly sensitive to how close his body was to hers. Sidestepping him, she put a few more feet between them and glanced at Elle. Annoyance rose up at the sight of her sitting next to Seth and watching him playing a stupid game.

Seriously? Wasn't she supposed to have Gwen's back?

Frustrated, she turned, only to find Markus several inches from her. Startled, she lost her balance and had to reach out and grab his biceps to steady herself. That was it. "What's your problem?"

The corner of his lips twitched. "I don't have a problem."

"Do you always crowd people?"

The twitch in his mouth turned into a grin. "No. Only you."

"Lucky me..." She stopped talking because his black eyes shimmered with flecks of blue, then his pupils lengthened until they looked like a cat's. Her pulse hammered under her skin and her breaths came in short gasps.

No. Those were not cat eyes.

"Dragon," she managed to whisper right before she bolted for the door.

But Markus was suddenly there, blocking her escape. Shaking all over and fighting to get her lungs to work right, she retreated hastily only stopping when Elle cupped her face. "Gwen. Breathe. In...out."

Gwen focused on her best friend and obeyed.

Without breaking eye contact, Elle spoke to Markus.

"I thought we were going to break the news to her calmly."

"It's done now. She doesn't fear me. She fears the image her mind created of the monster that killed her parents." Markus spoke from somewhere to her right.

Gwen pulled away from Elle and looked at the others standing around. *Sure, stare at the crazy lady.* "Are they all...dragons?"

Elle nodded. "But they won't hurt us."

Gwen shook her head and fled.

Markus gave Gwen a ten-minute head start. He could sense her, and she hadn't gone too far. Walking around the house, he found her sitting on one of the stone benches in the rose garden. Her head was tilted toward the night sky. Her creamy skin seemed to glow under the moonlight, and the sudden, irrational urge to caress her filled him.

What in Hades was wrong with him?

No matter how beautiful Gwen was, how perfectly she would fit tucked into his side and in his bed, he couldn't have her. Descendants were off limits. Zeus created that law the day he banned the Sons of War from the Heavens.

"Elle says you're not evil, that she doesn't sense a darkness in any of you. I trust her instincts." Gwen glanced over at him.

"We may not be up for saint of the year or anything, but we are not to be feared—at least not by you." Markus took a step forward and, when she didn't make a move to run, he continued until he stopped near her.

Edging sideways on the bench, she gestured for him to sit. "I'm sorry for freaking out."

"It's understandable."

She fell silent and he wondered what she was thinking and how much he should tell her. Aphrodite did tell him to guard Gwen. Did that mean he should tell her anything?

Did it matter? A rebellion brewed after all.

"Have you heard of the Sons of War?"

"I heard my father mention them once or twice. He said they were immortal warriors forged by the teeth of Ares's dragon…" When she stopped speaking, he glanced at her from the corner of his eye. She'd shifted to study him. "Legend says they betrayed Zeus and were sentenced to death."

Markus shrugged again. "Ares, our father, convinced Zeus that a more suitable punishment would be for us to live on Earth. It was Zeus who put us in charge of watching over the descendants to keep them from starting another war with the gods."

Gwen raised her brows. "And Zeus believed that the god of war wanted to stop a war?"

Markus smiled. "Ares, along with the other gods, likes the way things are. Besides, if the veil between the worlds fell, life as we know it would change. I don't have to tell you what a catastrophe that would be."

"No, I guess not." She fell silent again.

The faint roar of the ocean filled the silence as he watched her stare into the rose garden, illuminated by tiny multi-colored lights that ran around the edge of the flowerbeds. Her features were so much like Aphrodite, beautiful and divine. Unlike her goddess grandmother though, Gwen held him completely captive.

After what seemed like minutes, she turned back to him and they looked into each other's eyes for several moments before she broke the contact. With his perfect night vision he saw the blush in her cheeks.

That was better.

He stood and offered his hand. "Come, walk with me."

Hesitantly, she placed her hand in his and let him pull her to her feet. Linking their fingers, he headed down the path that weaved around the gardens. When she didn't pull away, his dragon calmed. Although a bittersweet longing rose within him, because he wanted her, yet couldn't—no, *shouldn't*—have her.

After a few feet, she said, "The gardens are beautiful."

"Aphrodite said an estate as big as ours deserved a garden. Ares thinks she overdid it."

"Are they a couple?"

A laugh escaped before he could contain it. "No.

Lovers? Maybe, but they aren't husband and wife, if that's what you're asking."

"I don't know. There are so many versions of their stories." She started to add something else, but stopped.

Silence filled the air as they continued their pace through the gardens. Her scent mingled with the smell of roses, a bouquet of sensuality and desire. The mission Aphrodite wanted him to go on didn't seem so bad. In fact, it was nice talking with her, watching her beautiful features change with each emotion as she spoke. "I have to confess that I'm not a very patient person. I'm only being so now because I find you intriguing."

Coming to a halt, she faced him, narrowing her eyes. "Why did you reveal yourself to me? Was it to prove to me that, no matter where I go, I can't escape the monster that torched my father while I was helpless to stop it?"

The sharp scent of her annoyance grew stronger every second he gazed into her sky blue eyes without responding. What he'd said was true. Patience wasn't his best virtue. Yet with Gwen, he could look at her all night, and listen to her talk for a lifetime.

"Well?" she clipped out when he didn't speak.

"Your grandmother asked me to protect you."

She shook her head. "I don't believe you. Why would she do that?"

"Because she is forbidden to have direct contact with you."

Confusion darkened her gaze and she shook her

head again. "Why? I'm her granddaughter. If she cared so much, she'd protect me, but she didn't."

When he stepped closer, her heart rate increased, but somehow he didn't think it was from fear. "I never lie. It is pointless for any of my brothers to lie. We cannot lie to one another. It's part of the curse that bans us from the Heavens."

Her eyes began to tear up. Damn, he'd fall to his knees and offer her anything if she started crying. It was his only weakness. It was one reason why Aphrodite came to him to watch over Gwen, that he was sure of.

"She let him die," she said on a sob.

A solitary tear fell. Reaching out, he cupped her face, and wiped the tear from her cheek with his thumb. Then he slowly lowered his head to brush his lips against hers. Gwen inhaled deeply, but didn't pull away. He closed the small gap between them and snaked an arm around her waist to draw her body flush against his while he deepened the kiss.

Her palms flattened on his chest, but she opened for him when he ran his tongue over her lips. Gods, she tasted like the Heavens. Sweet, like berries with a hint of mint. A growl rose from deep in his throat, and he moved his mouth with hers as their tongues brushed together in a sensual dance.

He slid his hands down her back and cupped her ass and lifted her feet off the ground. Instantly, she wrapped her legs around him and ground her core against his hard as hell cock that strained painfully into the zipper of his jeans.

The clearing of a throat broke the lust haze. Gwen wiggled out of his hold and he eased her down to her feet before he cast the intruder a glare.

Seth grinned. "Alfred says, 'Dinner is served.'" Then the dragon walked back to the house, laughing.

Bastard.

Gwen went to follow him, but Markus stopped her with a hand on her arm. He leaned in, and brushed his lips to her ear in a whisper. "We will continue this conversation later."

CHAPTER SIX

G wen sat at the small kitchen table looking out the opened window. The salty, slightly crisp, ocean breeze blew inside, kissing her cheeks. The quiet roar of the waves in the distance was like a soothing and peaceful melody.

Her thoughts kept wandering to the kiss she'd shared with Markus the night before and heat that rushed through every part of her body. One part of her wanted the man that sent her into a lust-crazed mess. The other part screamed for her to run from the dragon.

He was a dragon, a predator at the highest point on the food chain.

Elle sat down across from her at the table with a wide grin. "Are you going to share?"

"Nope"

"Fine, keep your dirty little secrets." Elle took a sip of her coffee then asked, "What's on the agenda today?"

"Markus is coming over to help me decipher my father's research notes."

"Do you think you'll find anything?"

Gwen shrugged. "I don't know. I hope so. I have so many unanswered questions surrounding Mom and Dad's deaths."

Elle reached over and covered her hand. "We'll find those answers, too. I really believe the dragons can help. And they could show us more about the world we truly belong in."

Gwen hoped so, too. She and Elle had never really fit in with the humans. Most just ignored them, but there were some who could sense they were different. Those people treated them like freaks. *Gods forbid anyone be a little different.*

The doorbell rang, stirring the butterflies in her belly and making her heart dance. Good gods. What was wrong with her?

The man was a dragon.

When she didn't move toward the door, Elle laughed and stood. "I'll get it."

"You do that." Gwen said back with a smile.

A few moments later, she heard the soft, deep rumble of Markus's voice drift in from the foyer right before he stepped into the kitchen. When she looked up at him, her breath caught. Damn, he looked too good to be a man-eating dragon.

Okay, so he wasn't a man-eating dragon. That she knew of, anyway.

She motioned for him to sit. "Would you like some coffee?"

Shaking his head, he took the offered seat. Their large kitchen suddenly shrank and became smaller. Averting her gaze, she looked out the window. "It's beautiful here."

"Yes."

His gaze on her felt like a physical touch and it made her antsy. Standing, she took her cup to the sink, rinsed it, and turned to face him. She gasped at the sight of him standing about a foot away. Gwen took a breath to calm her racing heart and to try to tamp down the desire building in her abdomen. "Should we go up to the office?"

"You have an office?"

"It's more like a studio-office. The third floor is a large open space and Elle is using half as her studio and I'm using the other half as an office." She stepped around him, careful not to touch. It wasn't that she was afraid of him, not after the kiss he laid on her last night. It was hard to fear a creature that made her hot in all the right ways.

Once upstairs, Gwen tried to put space between her and Markus. His presence was just too overwhelming, too much man. She inhaled deeply, and then wished she hadn't. His rich, spicy scent filled her senses.

Damn, she was in trouble.

Dragon. Oh fucking hell. Dragon or not, he was still

a man. Besides if he really wanted to hurt her, he wouldn't have kissed her last night.

Looking around, she tried to recall where she'd put the box. Then she remembered and whirled around and came face-to-face with Markus's chest. When she stumbled back a step, he gripped her elbow to help steady her. Her skin heated at his touch, and she eased out of his grasp and sidestepped him. "The box is over here."

About halfway to the box, she stepped on a board and it gave way under her foot. She let out a squeak as she fell, then cried out as sharp pain shot from her ankle up her leg. Markus was there in a flash, lifting her from the floor and setting her in a nearby chair.

Gently, he cupped her foot in his hand and frowned. "You're bleeding." Before she could respond, he removed her shoe and sock. When he took the hem of her jeans in his hands like he was going to rip the fabric, she yelled, "No!"

He froze. "What is it?"

"Don't rip them."

"Why? I need to see your wound. I'll buy you another pair of jeans." He ripped the pant leg up to her knee and she sighed.

"It's not the money. You know how hard it is to find that perfect pair of jeans?" At his look of confusion, she sighed. "No. Of course not."

Elle appeared at the top of the stairs, out of breath. "I heard a noise…" She stared at the hole in the floor and rushed over. "Oh, are you okay?"

Gwen nodded. "I'm fine. Can you go get the first aid kit?"

Elle nodded and disappeared only to return a moment later with the white box. She handed the box over to Markus, who opened it and proceeded to take care of her ankle.

"You know, I could do that."

"So can I."

Stubborn man.

When he had her leg cleaned and a bandage over the cut, he stood and scooped her up. "Hey, I can walk. I didn't break anything."

Instead of replying, he carried her toward the stairs.

"Wait. There's a black lockbox in the cardboard box on the desk."

To her relief, he turned to grab the box before continuing to the first floor.

Once settled on the couch with her feet in Markus's lap, she ignored the warmth that spread through her and unlocked the box. With a satisfied grin, she held up a flashdrive for Markus to see. "I don't suppose one of your brothers is a computer geek? Knowing my father, this could be encrypted."

Returning her smile, he said, "Zavier is, although I wouldn't call him that to his face."

"Noted." Hope blossomed. Maybe she would finally have answers. She shifted through papers, then picked up a spiral notebook and opened it. A slip of paper fell out, but it wasn't a whole sheet. She turned it over and gasped.

There were five names listed with addresses, all of which were women. Elle's and Gwen's names were at the top of the handwritten list. The handwriting was not her father's.

Her blood chilled and she started to shake. Their names were followed by three other women she'd never heard of.

Markus took the paper from her and read over the names. With a curse he stood, careful to place her injured foot on the sofa. "Can I take this?"

"Yes, sure. Those other women are in trouble like us, aren't they? "

"I'm not sure, yet. I need to go talk to my father."

Standing, she followed him to the door. "You know something. Tell me."

He turned and cupped her cheek. "When you left your last home, what did you do?"

"We burnt it down. My father said to never leave anything behind."

Markus gave a short nod. "Good. I'll be back as soon as I can. I'll explain then."

Crossing her arms, she glared at him. "Explain now."

"I'm not sure. I must go talk to my father. Don't leave the house until I get back." Then he stepped out the door and rushed to his car and drove off.

Damn stubborn man.

MARKUS STORMED into his office about fifteen minutes later and summoned the god of war. "Ares! Show yourself."

The god materialized a few feet to Markus's left. "Is that any way to talk to your father?"

"You know anything about this?" Markus held out the piece of paper.

Ares snatched the paper and studied it. "No."

Markus grabbed the page back from Ares and sent a mental call to Zavier. Telepathic communication was part of the bond they created after falling from Olympus.

A few moments later, Zavier walked in and nodded once to Ares. Markus handed him the paper along with the flashdrive Gwen had given him. "The flashdrive belonged to Gwen's father. She said it could be encrypted. See if you can break the code, and check out the other names on the list."

Zavier raised a brow at Markus. "Gwen and Elle's names are on here."

"Yes. That makes me wonder if the other females on there are descendants as well."

"What would Gwen's father being doing with the list?"

Markus turned to Ares. "That's what I want to know."

Ares sat in Markus's leather chair behind his desk.

"How would I know? I don't keep track of Garrick's business or whom he works with. In fact, I don't give a shit what he does."

Markus growled. "That's bullshit. You said the descendants couldn't create another army. That is exactly what Garrick is doing."

"*Gary* is becoming a huge pain in my ass." Ares emphasized the nickname Seth used to piss off their brother. "He has been off my radar for a while now. I was hoping you would be able to track him down by now."

"Us? You're the mighty god of war and you can't find your own son?" Markus slammed his hands down on the desk.

"Your female will bring him to you." Ares leaned forward so that they were nose-to-nose.

Markus jerked back and began to pace. "So help me, Ares…tell me what you know."

"Those names are only part of a list. My guess is Garrick has a lot more names than just those five. However, it is interesting that Tom Preston got the names. It may be why your brother killed him." Ares rose from the chair and walked around the desk. "Oh, and Markus? Don't forget the curse. You cannot have your female without a sacrifice."

Ares vanished.

"Fuck." Markus roared and turned to Zavier, who sat at the small round table with his laptop. The male's brows were drawn together as he studied the screen.

That wasn't very promising. Markus walked over to peer over Zavier's shoulder. "What is it?"

"I've never seen this code before. It's going to take a while to decipher."

Markus fisted his hands at his side. "Make it your priority. I have a feeling Tom Preston was in deeper than Gwen knew."

"Got it." Zavier closed the laptop and stood. "I'm going to take this up to my office. I also got a report a few moments before you arrived that there's been an angel sighting in the village."

Markus let another F bomb fly and ran a hand through is hair. "What now? I'll get Ty and go check it out."

If the humans saw what they believed to be an angel, Markus was betting it was most likely a descendant that'd came into his powers. Which meant Garrick had sent out scouts to search for Gwen and Elle.

Markus had to take care of the scout, then go pack up Gwen and Elle and move them into the estate whether they liked it or not.

CHAPTER SEVEN

In dragon form, Markus touched down at the base of the mountain, several yards from Serenity Cove. He and his brothers owned the secluded patch of land and had it warded so humans couldn't see them land or take off in dragon form. Even though many of the elders of the village knew what they were, the tourist trade that provided the small town with most of its income didn't. Markus preferred it that way. They weren't circus freaks and didn't want to take the chance of humans treating them as such.

Markus folded his wings as he focused on his human form and shifted, conjuring clothes to cover his body at the same time. The Sons of War weren't gods, but immortal warrior dragons-shifters who possessed their own magic, which rivaled the power of the gods.

A moment later Ty landed and shifted to his human form and rolled his shoulders as they walked toward the center of the small fishing village. "This better be good. I haven't had a decent workout in years."

Markus couldn't agree more. Their father's desire to fight burned in their veins. Unlike Ares, Markus kept a tight lid on the part of him that longed to create wars and conflict.

Letting out a low growl, Markus said, "If the descendants are showing their abilities and, in this case, their wings in public, then we'll get the fight we long for."

The demi-gods, who'd inherited feather-like wings from their divine ancestors, were often called angels by the humans who saw them. Markus could understand the confusion. After all, myths of winged creatures and beings with godly powers were only fairytales they told their children.

They'd rounded the corner to the docks when Markus stopped and placed a hand on Ty's chest, halting his brother. Markus nodded his head and Ty smiled at what he saw. "Well, isn't he pretty?"

The male had long, white feather-like wings he wasn't even trying to hide. Markus searched their surroundings and inhaled. The only scents he picked up on were the salt from the ocean, the fish from the boats, various foods from the area restaurants, and the descendent. The power rolling off the male told him he was one of Garrick's minions. Imperials, they called themselves, as though they were above all laws. Markus suspected that this Imperial wasn't alone.

Ty growled low so only Markus could hear. "I smell a trap."

"Yep. It wouldn't be fun any other way."

Ty chucked. "Well, let's get this party started."

They advanced on the male. When they got within a couple of feet, the descendant smiled and took off toward town center. Markus and Ty gave chase and the townspeople darted out of their way. Many of the residents of Serenity Cove knew about the "dragons in the castle." Most viewed Markus and his brothers as guardians of a sort—a rumor Markus happily allowed to flourish. It was easier to live with humans who didn't fear them.

They chased the demi-god to the edge of town. The male turned toward them and thrust an energy bolt at Ty. The bolt struck him in the chest, knocking him back several feet. Ty landed on his back and slid until he hit the side of a building.

Briefly stunned, Ty surged to his feet, shook off the effects, and let out a roar that shook the buildings around them. Then he ran toward the descendant and shifted into his red and gold dragon about halfway to the male. The man paled as he stretched out his wings and took to the air.

Not missing a beat, Ty swooped up to follow. Cursing, Markus shifted and joined his brother. The last thing he needed was for Ty to kill the demi-god before they got some answers.

The little bastard's fast, Ty said in thought.

Markus's reply was a grunt as he jerked upward to avoid power lines the winged asshat flew under. Markus was a millisecond from telling Ty to light the demigod's ass on fire when the descendent finally landed on the stretch of beach between the estate and Gwen and Elle's lighthouse.

As soon as he and Ty landed and shifted to their human forms, three more descendants materialized.

Garrick must have found a way to unlock their powers. Markus growled, keeping the conversation with his brother telepathic.

And you're surprised by that?

Ignoring Ty's sarcasm, Markus charged the two closest to him while Ty followed suit. Animal instincts gave him and his brothers the advantage of better vision, hearing, and speed. It was yet another thing the gods feared. The Sons of War were faster and stronger, even without the magic they inherited from their father.

Markus punched the first descendant, a blond male, before the man could register the movement. Then Markus swung his leg out, catching another male in the back of the legs. The second male screamed and fell to his knees in the sand.

Searing pain exploded across Markus's back, knocking him to the ground. Rage filled his veins and he twisted around to see the blond male charging at him. Markus flung his arm back just as the descendant reached him, grabbed the male by the arm and jerked him forward. The male flipped over Markus and landed hard on his back. Fisting his hand, Markus swung and hit the bastard in the jaw. He heard a crack as his knuckles made contact. The male's head whipped to the side, out cold.

Pushing to his feet, Markus scanned the beach for more descendants. His gaze landed on a photo half buried in the sand. Picking it up, his heart skipped several beats. Rage burned within him, fueling the dragon's protectiveness over the female in the picture.

Gwen.

They were here to find her.

Markus whirled around and almost ran into Ty. With a growl, Markus thrust the photo into Ty's hand. "We need to move the females to the estate. Now." Shifting, he took to the air and flew toward the lighthouse and Gwen, knowing Ty would call Drake and Seth in to do clean up.

GWEN PLACED her wine glass on the table and considered opening the black lockbox that contained her father's research documents and notes. Hovering her hand over the container, she wondered what had her so hesitant to go through the contents. It wasn't like she was violating his privacy, yet she felt she doing just that. He'd want her to know the truth about the Sons of War and her life, wouldn't he?

Of course. Gods, she was being silly and a chicken.

A knock sounded on the front door as she lifted the lid. It was barely four o'clock in the afternoon, and she wasn't expecting anyone—though it could be Markus. Reaching out, she closed the box and locked it before heading to the door. When she got there, she hesitated. A cold chill skated up her spine and made the hairs on the back of her neck stand on end.

A peek through the peephole revealed a man she didn't know. Sliding the chain into place, she opened the door and spoke through the small crack. "Yes?"

The stranger smiled. "Hello. Are you Miss Preston?"

Warning bells rang inside her head while her gut tightened with fear. "No. I'm afraid not." Closing the door, she whirled around to see Elle step off the staircase.

Gwen placed her finger over her mouth and indicated to the back door. They started to move just as the front windows shattered, spraying glass all over the living room. Gwen ran, only to be jerked back by her hair and tossed to the ground. A large man towered over her and kicked her in the side. Pain exploded in her ribs and shot down her body, making her cry out.

The man leaned down to grab a handful of her hair and pulled her to her feet with a tug on her already aching scalp. He yanked her into him and she could feel his arousal against her stomach through their clothes. Bile rose in her throat and she took shallow breaths to keep from being sick.

When his lips touched her cheek, she lost the ability

to reason. Jerking her knee up, hard, she slammed it into him in the balls. The man cried out and let go of her. Gwen took that opportunity to kick him again, this time in the back as he curled in a fetal position on the floor.

Elle screamed, and Gwen saw her sister fly across the room and hit the wall. Fury raged inside Gwen and she charged the man who dared hurt her. Gwen hit him in the gut and they fell to the floor. Sitting on his chest, she managed to get a few good punches in before she was flipped on her back. The man straddled her, grinned, and raised his fist. Closing her eyes, she braced for the impact. A loud boom sounded close by. Then the man was gone.

Gwen opened her eyes and saw the monster from her dreams. A huge black dragon stood in the center of her living room. Terror overtook her. Her breathing turned into short gasps as a panic attack took hold like a vise around her lungs. Desperate to protect her sister, she raced backwards on her hands and knees until she reached Elle and pulled her into a hug.

"So sorry," she said into Elle's hair. The panic and fear erupted into uncontrollable tears as she rocked back and forth with Elle.

A warm hand touched her arm, she screamed, and backed further into the corner with Elle. Markus appeared in her line of sight. She blinked and hoped her vision wasn't playing tricks on her.

"Gwen. You're safe now."

She shook her head. "Dragon."

Markus held out his hand, but didn't touch her. "It was me."

"It was the black dragon. The one that—"

"It was me. My dragon is black and blue."

Sifting through the hazy memories, she couldn't remember the undertone of the dragon. All she saw was black and her mind instantly returned to the night when she watched her father burn to death because of the damned black dragon.

"Gwen? You're safe now." Markus repeated, drawing her attention back to him. He slid his fingers around her wrist and urged her to release Elle. "Come on. I'm going to take you two back the estate. You and Elle need medical attention."

Gwen took a shaky breath and allowed Markus to take Elle from her arms. When he turned, she saw Zavier and Ty behind him. Markus handed Elle to Zavier, who cradled her with such gentleness that Gwen relaxed a little.

Markus lifted her from the floor and held her to his chest. His rich, spicy scent enveloped her, erasing the terror that threatened to consume her. It was ironic how she could find such comfort in the very creature she'd run from for so long.

CHAPTER EIGHT

Ash fisted her hands at her side as she watched the three dragons help the women inside the black Range Rover. She'd arrived too late. The black dragon —Markus, she believed was his name—had already ripped through the lighthouse and the Imperials like they were no more than wooden toys.

Suddenly, the one who wore the sunglasses all the time stopped with his hand hovering next to the driver's side door handle, and jerked his head in her direction. *Shit.* Her heart dropped to her feet at the intensity of his expression.

Fleeing before he made her, she materialized inside the small apartment she'd rented under her mother's name. Well, her mother's human name since she couldn't very well use Artemis as her alias.

The dragon shouldn't have been able to sense her, or see her. Yet the way he stared in her direction, where she stood cloaked from sight by a spell, felt as if he looked right at her. *Impossible.* Not even Garrick could sense her in that state.

Not able to fully trust the dragon, she'd spied on him for years. Something about him didn't sit right. Of course, Garrick was a charmer and easy on the eyes, but there was a darkness surrounding him. His obsession with his brothers only added to her suspicions.

Ash had decided to get to the bottom of the obsession and see what it was about the other five dragons that had Garrick shaking in his undies.

Her phone rang and she glanced at the screen and groaned when she saw it was Garrick. *Fucking great. What now?*

"Your Imperials are weak," she said in greeting.

"Hello to you too, love."

His arrogant tone rubbed her nerves raw and she took a deep breath to try to calm herself. "You underestimated your brothers."

That got his attention. Ash smiled as Garrick growled through the phone. "I do not acknowledge them as kin of mine. I didn't underestimate anyone. You did."

"Me? I told you to send me your best. I set up a distraction. The females were alone. You'd think your demi-gods in full possession of their powers could capture them." Ash was fuming. It was so like him to push the blame on her.

"Yes, however, they are five dragons and can communicate telepathically."

"I know. I'm not stupid."

"I never said you were." He fell silent for a moment before asking, "What is your next move, huntress?"

"I'm working on it."

After shutting off her phone before he could reply to her tart words, she shoved the thing into her back packet. What she needed was more information on the Sons of War and she knew just how to get it.

GWEN SAT on the sofa and sifted through her father's notes while Markus and his brothers discussed the attacks. There was more growling going on than talking, although she tried to block out most of their conversation. It was all so surreal—being protected by the same creatures that killed her father.

Well not *the* same dragon. Just the same species.

Lifting her gaze, she watched Markus pace in front of the others. His larger frame stalked gracefully and powerfully back and forth across the living room floor. His short, black hair stood on end from the multiple times he'd run his hands through it. It made him look sexier. Like he just rolled out of bed. How would it feel to run her fingers through the dark strands?

As if sensing her attention, Markus stopped. Her cheeks warmed at his steady regard, and she returned her attention to the lockbox. A photo peeking out from under a small leather bound notebook caught her attention. Picking it up, she sucked in a breath and started to tremble.

"What is it?" Markus knelt in front of her in an instant.

Gwen turned the picture around to show him. "This is the man who killed my father."

Markus worked his jaw as if he were clenching his teeth together and took the photo. Removing the notebook, she found several more photos beneath it. Some of Markus and his brothers, some of her father, and one of *that man* and her father together, smiling like they were friends.

Her vision blurred. Half-blinded by anger and grief, she passed the photo to Markus. "My father knew him. I don't understand. Is that you brother?"

Markus studied the picture, brows drawn together. "Yes. That man with your father is Garrick."

"Why would my father be with him, smiling like they were BFFs?" A tremor passed through her, leaving her cold and confused. Why would her father get involved with someone like Garrick? She wouldn't believe it, *couldn't* believe it.

Markus laid the picture down, gripped her hands, and held them. "Garrick is very convincing. It is possible your father didn't know who or what he was when this picture was taken."

None of this made sense to her. "The night my parents were killed, there were three men, Garrick being one of them. They were searching the house for something. Do you know what they were looking for? Why he killed my parents?"

Markus squeezed her hands gently and took a deep breath. "Garrick is building an army of descendants and plans to wage war against the gods."

Her heart sank. "My father would had never got involved with anything like that."

Zavier spoke next from the chair next to her. "Tom must have found out and turned on Garrick. It's could be why Garrick killed him."

Gwen agreed with Zavier's logic. There was no way her father would associate with someone like Garrick if he knew his true purpose. Yet, she couldn't dismiss the evidence inside the box on her lap—the notes about the gods, the descendants, Garrick and the other Sons of War. It pointed to the possibility that her father worked with or under Garrick's command at one time.

The feel of the box being lifted out of her lap brought her out of the disturbing thoughts. She met Markus's midnight blue eyes as he closed the lockbox and set it on the sofa next to her. Then he stood, taking her hand and pulling her to her feet. "Where are we going?"

"For a walk."

Images of the hot-as-hell kiss the night before flashed in her mind. Her pulse kicked up and she started to pull away from Markus when he leaned in and whispered in her ear. "I'll behave."

Pressing her lips together to keep from smiling, she

studied him for a moment, then shook her head. "I'll hold you to that."

A low chuckle served as his answer. He led her from the living room, then out the large kitchen to a door that opened to the side yard. The cool, salty, night air hit her. Overhead stars glittered against the sky like diamonds on a black canvas. "It's a beautiful night."

"Yes. Are you cold?"

Gwen shook her head. Her heart stilled for a brief moment as they stopped a foot away from the edge. It was too dark for her to see where she was going. Fear at the lack of control sparked a small panic attack. She took deep breaths to try to calm herself, but it was no use. Damn it, she should be past this. In fact, she thought she'd been coping well until those descendants showed up at her house and she saw Markus in dragon form.

The combination had thrust her into the past, left her watching helplessly as her father burned to death. His screams still haunted her.

"Gwen."

Markus's cool, commanding tone brought her back to the present. He cradled her face in his hands, but she couldn't make out his eyes in the shadows. Suddenly, specks of blue appeared and seemed to glow as they grew larger until the lighter blue drowned out the darker color before they transformed into the eyes of Markus's dragon. Unlike the first time she saw the change, she didn't fear it. Instead, the sight calmed her.

"Gwen," Markus said again. This time it was huskier, almost a growl.

"I'm here. Do you always growl?"

Another lower, sexier sounding, rumble came from him, making her shiver. "Yes. Why did you have another attack?"

Even though he spoke softly, she heard the undercurrent of a demand in his tone. Needing some space, she stepped away from him only to have him wrap an arm around her waist and jerk her into his hard, too hot body. Surprised, she grabbed his biceps. "Hey."

"We're close to the edge." He whispered in her ear, his lips brushing against her lobe and making her shiver. "Look down."

She did and gasped. They were about a foot away from where the cliff fell away, but that wasn't what stole her breath. The village below was lit up. The streetlights mapped out the town's layout perfectly from this height. The docks were alive with boats coming and going.

"It's beautiful."

"I love to sit along the edge of the cliff and just watch. They're good people."

Gwen's heart warmed at his offer of a private thought, and an endearing confession. Trust. "I have the power of persuasion." It wasn't the best of confessions, but it was her only secret.

Markus stilled and she could feel his gaze on her. "Who knows of your power?"

"Just Elle and my parents. I haven't used it since high school."

"You have control over it, then?"

Fear crept back within her and she stepped back. "Yes. Why do you ask?"

When he reached for her, she jerked away and lost her footing. The earth collapsed under her and she screamed as she began to fall. In the next instant, she was cradled against Markus's chest.

Wrapping her arms around his waist, she pressed her head to his chest, and allowed the rapid *thump*, *thump* of his heart to sooth her own racing pulse.

Markus kissed her temple. "I'm sorry. You mustn't be afraid of me. I could never harm you, even if I wanted to."

What? Wait, did he want to hurt her, or was it something else entirely? "What are you saying?"

"You're my mate."

The words were spoken so low, she almost missed them. Was he serious? His mate. She shook her head. "I can't. I mean, I don't know you."

"Not yet. But you can't stop the mating once it's begun."

Still shaking her head, unable to grasp what he was saying, she stared at him. She couldn't mate a dragon. She knew nothing about him.

You could get to know him.

The words sounded like a whisper in the breeze,

startling Gwen. Jerking her head up, she searched their dark surroundings. "Is there someone here? A woman?"

Markus shook his head. "No, why?"

"I thought I heard...oh, never mind. I've had too much excitement for one day and now I'm hearing things." Needing to be alone, to think and absorb everything that had happened in the last twenty-four hours, she tried to step around him. He blocked her path. She searched his face and sighed. "I'm tired."

Instead of responding, he stared back at her. Even though it was a dark moonless night, her eyes had adjusted enough she could barely make out the hard lines and those full, masculine lips.

In the next instant, his mouth pressed against hers and his tongue demanded entrance. Defeat washed over her and she found it impossible to deny him. Her body responded to him in a way it never had with anyone else, no other lover made her burn like Markus did.

And all with a single touch.

Gwen moaned as she opened to allow his tongue entrance. Markus snaked his arms around her waist and pressed their bodies together. Her skin felt tight and like it was on fire. She shouldn't encourage him, shouldn't be allowing him to kiss her, to touch her. He was a dragon, the son of Ares, and dangerous.

Yet, she wanted more of him. No, she *craved* more. It was crazy. They just met.

Breaking the kiss, he bent down to slide an arm under her legs and picked her up. Not expecting the sudden movement, she squeaked, then covered her mouth. His soft chuckle filled her ears before he spoke. "You are mine, Gwen. I'm not letting you go."

She swallowed. When he started walking toward the house, she asked, "Where are you taking me?"

"To bed."

Her belly flipped. "No. I mean…I can't."

He laughed. "To sleep. You're tired and need to sleep."

"Oh." Now she felt embarrassed and a little disappointed. Man, she was a mess when it came to Markus. She was also in jeopardy of losing her heart to the man, or having it broken into a billion pieces.

Yep, she was in deep.

CHAPTER NINE

G wen woke to the soft sounds of music. Yawning, she sat up in the king size bed and looked around the room. *Markus's bed and room.*

The room was huge and beautiful in a masculine kind of way. Dark green drapes with sheer cream-colored curtains hung from ceiling to floor, the furniture elegantly hand carved cherry oak.

Flinging the covers away, she swung her legs over the side of the bed. The house was quiet and she wondered if she was the only one awake as she stood up and walked to the bathroom. Once inside she gasped. The thing was bigger than her bedroom in Nebraska.

A huge garden tub sat next to a walk-in shower big enough for ten people. Turning to the dual sink vanity, she considered herself in the mirror and frowned. Her blond bedhead hair surrounded her face and slightly puffy eyes. "What are you doing, Gwen?"

She should leave. But where else could she run to and be safe from Garrick?

All she'd done for the last fourteen years was run from her demons. Rather the dragon that wanted to use her in ploy to wage war on the gods.

No, she was tired of running. It'd gotten her nowhere. Besides, no matter where she went, they always found her.

It was time for her to face her fears and learn how to kick their asses.

Exiting the bathroom, she searched the room for something to throw over her T-shirt and panties. Her gaze stopped on a royal blue robe draped over a chair next to the window. That would do. She tugged it on before heading downstairs.

MUFFLED voices came from a closed door across the foyer. Crossing the space, she knocked on the door, hoping to find Markus. The door jerked opened to reveal Ty. She swallowed, then took a deep breath. "I'm looking for Markus."

Ty grunted and stepped aside. Markus sat behind a large cherry oak desk. Drake was perched across from him with a tablet in his hand. The men swiveled their gazes to her at the same time.

Without meaning to, she took a step back. Light blue rippled through Markus's dark irises, making her pulse spike.

Damn it. She needed to get over her fear.

Markus leaned back in his chair. "Leave us."

Drake let out a low growl, but stood and walked out of the room. Ty nudged her inside and whispered, "Have fun," before he closed the door, shutting her in with Markus.

"Come here, Gwen."

With steady steps, she walked over to his desk and claimed the chair Drake abandoned. Taking a deep, calming breath, she met his gaze. "I want you to teach me to fight."

His eyes did the color shift thing again and she suppressed a shiver. "Why?"

"Because I want to help."

"Help with what?"

Annoyed, she pursed her lips and studied him. His dark brows raised in challenge. Was he trying to irritate her? "I think you know what I'm talking about."

"I have my suspicions. Speak your mind. I don't bite." He leaned over the desk. "Unless you want me to."

Gwen's cheeks heated and she imagined they turned every shade of red. This man knew how to push every one of her sensory buttons without even touching her.

Steeling her back and gathering all the courage she could, she met and held his gaze. "I want to help destroy the man—er, dragon—who killed my parents. I want you to teach me how."

He sat back, brows drawn together in one harsh line.

His forehead creased as if he were angry, but she couldn't tell if it was her request or the reminder of what his brother had done to her family that made him mad.

"I don't think so."

Her own fury rose. "You don't think what?"

"You're not fighting in this war. I'm not discussing it any further." Then he turned to his computer and started typing.

Shock and annoyance froze her place for a second. How dare he dismiss her as if she were weak? Sure, she let her fears control her for far too long, but she was trying to get past that. Buried anger surfaced, fueling her newly formed backbone. Coming to her feet, she slammed her hands down on his desk.

"I *am* discussing it and you're going to listen to me. I'm not a helpless woman to be pushed aside while the *men* take care of the monsters." The ability to breathe became a little harder, and she shook. Markus turned off the computer, rose and towered over her. It didn't do anything to calm her mood. "Oh, no. You will not try to intimidate me. I'm serious. I want your brother dead and I want to be there to see it happen."

Grief and rage consumed her and her eyes started to water.

Markus reached out with a hand, but she slapped it away and turned her back on him. Damn, she would not start crying. Not now.

"Training you to fight will take some time. You'll have to build up your strength and learn how to use multiple weapons, because the only weapon that can kill one of us is in located in the Underworld."

Seriously, they had a weapon that could kill Garrick? Glancing over her shoulder, she narrowed her eyes at him. "Then go get it."

A frown formed on his lips and his forehead creased. "Yeah, right. Hades doesn't allow people to enter the Underworld with an extended stay pass. And he's even less likely to just hand over the dagger."

Facing, she crossed her arms. "Then we find out how to kill him or at least get close enough to behead him."

Walking around his desk, he stopped inches from her. Her heart hammered frantically, but she stood her ground and straightened her spine. "Are you going to teach me to fight or am I going to see if one of your brothers will? I bet Seth would."

He let out a growl and slid an arm around her waist. Good. She hoped Seth would be the trigger that got his attention. It was unclear how she knew, but she sensed Seth was the more sensual brother. The one who went on the prowl a little too often—maybe her connection to Aphrodite served her more than she'd thought.

"You will not be training with Seth."

She raised her brows. "Then are you going to do it?"

"On one condition." His lips twitched, but his eyes still held aggression.

"What?" She swallowed, hard.

"You do exactly what I say to do. No whining or arguing."

She nodded. "Agreed."

Smiling, he added, "One more thing. You will meet me for a private dinner every night until I say otherwise."

She stilled and studied him for a few moments. He was serious. Although the thought of having dinner with him every night both intrigued and frightened the hell out of her. "Okay, but I want my own bedroom."

With a raised brow, he transformed his smile to wicked grin. "I don't think so."

Shit. There was no resisting him when she had to spend the evenings with him. She might as well cut out her heart now and offer it up on a silver platter.

MARKUS CUPPED the back of Gwen's head and pressed his lips to hers. A surprised gasp escaped her. He used that to thrust his tongue into her mouth, filling her the only way he dared. What he really wanted to do was throw her over his desk and bury his cock deep inside her.

A crash from the foyer made him break the kiss.

With a deep growl, he released Gwen's waist, grabbed her hand, and tugged her to the study door. He yanked it open and froze.

Maxwell, their butler for more than a century, stood

holding up a female, who was bleeding from her side. Long red hair caked with dirt blocked her face. Behind him Gwen gasped and pulled her hand from his. When she tried to go to the woman, Markus gripped her upper arm, stopping her.

Gwen stared at him, still angry with him. "She needs medical attention."

"Are you a doctor?"

Letting out a feminine, yet human growl, she jerked out of his hold to go to the woman. Markus was quick on her heels. He stopped within arm's reach of Maxwell and the woman, hooked a finger under her chin and lifted it so he could peer into her face. The moment he touched her skin, he felt her power reach out to his.

Fuck. This wasn't good.

She was a descendent, and her powers had been unlocked.

"Who did this to you?"

Meeting Markus's glance, she took a breath, then winced as if it hurt to breath. "Hunters…"

Gwen touched his arm, drawing his attention away from the descendent. "Please, can we get her medical attention? Then you can question her."

Just then Ty skidded into the room. "Fuck me."

Markus turned to him and frowned. Ty stood in the archway between the foyer and the great room staring at the woman. Anger, confusion, hurt, and a hint of compassion flashed over his features in a rapid slideshow of emotions.

Looking back at the woman, Markus noted how she glanced back at Ty as if he'd bite her without a moment's notice. She was right to be leery of him. Ty was not the gentlest of men.

"Sire?" Maxwell said in his British accent.

Markus gave a short nod and stepped forward to take the female from the butler, but Ty beat him to it. Markus's brother didn't say a word, simply lifted the woman in his arms and started up the stairs.

Markus followed and heard Gwen's light footsteps behind him. Not bothering to tell her to stay put, he let her come.

His curiosity spiked when Ty entered the room next to his and laid the woman on the bed. A moment later one of the two nymphs that took care of the house-keeping entered the room and quickly went to work on assisting the woman.

Thea and Ariel were gifts from Aphrodite—two of her best nymphs—and were very loyal and helpful in many ways. The female nymphs were born on Olympus and could aid in healing mortal wounds. They could also cook, which most likely saved he and his brothers' lives on more than one occasion.

Thea turned to them, her ice blue eyes accusing, and gestured for them to back up. "Give us room, please."

Ty growled, only making Thea fold her arms over her chest and glared at him. After a moment she sighed. "Trust us, dragon. We will not harm your female."

Something flashed over his features too fast for

Markus to gauge what it was. Ty took a step toward Thea. "She is not my female."

Thea rolled her eyes and went back to tending the woman's wounds.

Once they'd cleaned her up, Ariel stopped at the door and glanced back at Markus. "Her name is Ashlynn, and she's Artemis's daughter."

For all that is holy and then some. Markus was speechless as he studied the peacefully resting Ashlynn. This was not happening. A first generation demi-goddess with her full powers just so happened to stumble into their home by chance? He thought not.

"Ty, gather the others. We need to decide what to do with the female." Markus had his suspicions about her and her loyalty to her mother.

CHAPTER TEN

Markus sat at the corner bar in the great room and downed a shot of bourbon. "My first thought was she works with Garrick and was sent here to spy on us."

Next to him Drake sat with a beer in his hand. "I agree. Why else would she have come into her powers? Only the gods themselves can unlock a descendant's powers."

Across the room, Seth spoke from the oversized armchair. "Whoever stabbed her also beat her. Maybe she escaped."

Ty shook his head. "I don't like her here. She needs to leave."

Raking his fingers through his hair, Markus blew out a breath and wished he'd told Zavier to sit in on this meeting instead of babysitting Ashlynn. "I hear each of you and understand. But we can't just let her leave. She could very well run straight to Garrick and expose Gwen and Elle."

Drake set his beer down on the bar top hard enough the sound echoed through the downstairs of the estate. "As much as I don't like it, I have to agree. Therefore, she stays. We'll have to make her talk and keep an eye on her."

"We can't watch her 24/7." Ty snorted.

Markus met his brother's gaze and felt his lips lift on one side. "No, but she will not leave the house. You will be in charge of that."

Ty opened his mouth, then closed it before he turned and stormed out the room.

Setting his drink glass down, Markus stood. "I'll see if Gwen can help get the female to talk."

It was Drake who asked, "What makes you so sure she'd talk to Gwen?"

Without turning around, he replied, "Because she's a female and I am confident that Gwen could get Ashlynn to talk." Markus exited the living room before his brothers could ask any more questions. His main focus turned to Gwen, who was in a room with a female he didn't know or trust and with Zavier. Although out of all Markus's brothers, Z was the one he confided in the most.

There were boundaries that they'd never cross with each other. Gwen was one of those boundaries.

He opened the bedroom door and surveyed the room. Ashlynn slept peacefully in the bed. In the far corner of the room, Zavier and Gwen huddled over a laptop, their chairs so close together that the arms touched.

A growl escaped Markus, drawing both their heads up. Zavier shifted the laptop so it sat in front of him and slid his chair away from Gwen.

Gwen, however, just glared at him for a moment, then pointed at the computer and said, "Zavier broke my father's code."

Markus stared at her, not believing how unaffected by his aggression she'd become in such a short time.

Zavier stood, closed the laptop and turned to Gwen. "I'll load the files to a spare tablet so you can read them."

"Thank you." She offered him a warm smile.

Z nodded once, then left the room.

Gwen stood and started toward the door. Markus grabbed her arm, stopping her and making her meet his gaze. A hint of fear passed over her expression, but it was gone almost as fast as it appeared. A sense of joy fluttered in his chest and he smiled. Could she be trying to trust him?

"Go change into more comfortable clothes and meet me in the basement."

She pulled out of his grasp and took a step back. "Why?"

"Because you are about to have your first lesson in self-defense."

"I took self-defense classes. I need to know how to fight a dragon."

Leaning in, he growled, "Basement. Ten minutes."

Before he did something stupid, like haul her to his bedroom and pleasure her until she screamed his name, he left the room, annoyance running heavy in his veins.

That female was going to kill him before the week was up.

GWEN STORMED into the giant gym in the basement, and let the door slam shut behind her. The gym took up a little more than half of the length of the mansion. Markus had told her that the other half of the basement was Zavier's playground—in other words, a computer and security room. However, Z offered to share his space with Elle, turning half of the space into her own studio.

About two feet inside, she froze. Markus stood with his back facing her in the middle of the room, shirtless and wearing a pair of joggers that conformed to his tight ass and thighs. She swallowed. Slowly, he turned to face her and her heart skipped a beat. His face was set in hard lines and his eyes bored into her like a lion—or rather a dragon with his prey.

"Come here, Gwen."

She had to force her feet to move, but was proud that she actually managed to square her shoulders and make her way to him. As she stopped in front of him, he took a deep breath and briefly closed his eyes.

"You will need to relax. Your fear and anxiety only make me want you more."

The thought never crossed her mind. Of course he'd be driven by scent, his inner beast was a predator. By the way he focused on her and took slow even breaths, she knew he was battling his dragon and instinct to chase.

And she wanted to spar with the dragon.

Good gods, she must be insane for wanting to challenge one of the beasts from her nightmares.

"Give me your hand," he said in a husky tone.

She did as he commanded without question. When he caught her hand, she couldn't hold back a soft groan at the contact. Her skin tingled and warmed where he touched it. The heat traveled up her arm to spread through her whole body.

Meeting his intense stare, she somehow knew he felt the same thing. Yet neither of them spoke. Instead, Markus grabbed a roll of white tape and proceeded to wrap her hands like a boxer would.

Curious, she watched how his hands tenderly glided over and under hers as he worked.

After both hands were wrapped, Markus gripped her shoulders and turned her around until she faced a large sand bag hanging from the ceiling. He stepped around her and stood behind the bag. "You need to build your strength first and learn how to hit your target."

Narrowing her gaze, she propped her fist on her hips. "I know how to hit."

His lips lifted along with one dark brow. "Prove it."

She made a low growl-like sound in her throat and narrowed her eyes at him. "Make sure you hold onto that bag."

An hour later she stood under the hot sprays of the shower, and her whole body ached. Markus was insane.

And brutal.

Every muscle in her body had a work out, he made sure of it. After she finished several rounds with the punching bag, he switched her to the treadmill where he increased the speed and the incline every couple of minutes. Just when she thought he couldn't torture her any more, he broke out the yoga mats.

Now she liked yoga, and had spent many hours a week flexing and stretching her muscles, but the crap Markus had her do was not yoga. It was more like twister, by herself, with no spotted mat.

The man was crazy and trying to kill her.

A knock sounded on the bathroom door, making her groan. "Go away you, evil man."

"Meet me in the gardens when you're done." There was a laugh in that statement. Okay, so he wasn't evil like his brother Garrick was, but he had seemed to enjoy every torturous exercise he put her through.

She turned off the shower and got out, feeling a lot better than before. It was only the beginning. Her muscles were going to be stiff and sore in the morning. Letting out a sigh, she dried off then went out into the bedroom—Markus's bedroom—to search for clothes.

Deciding that she'd rather be comfortable, she picked out a pair of black leggings and an oversized red sweater, and then headed down to the gardens where she and Markus had shared their first kiss.

She shook that thought off. This was only dinner. It didn't matter that she had to share a bedroom with him —she wasn't sharing the bed.

Stepping out into the cool night air, Gwen drew in a breath, taking in the smells of ocean and sand. It was heavenly. Making the move to Maine had been a wonderful decision. Running was no longer an option, because she'd done enough of it in the last fourteen years. It was time she took control of her life and fight back.

The rose garden was full of fragrant, beautiful blooms and she made her way down the stone path. When she reached the center, she saw Markus dressed in a pair of black slacks and a white dress shirt. His dark, naturally tanned skin against the white cotton made him look sexier than ever.

Turning his head, he raised a brow at her and smiled. "You look lovely."

"I was going for comfy." She frowned.

"That, too." He chuckled and held out his hand.

When she placed a hand in his, he drew her closer, brought her knuckles to his mouth, and pressed a firm, but soft kiss on them. "Maxwell has set up a table and chairs for dinner out here."

"Maxwell?"

"The butler."

"Seth called him Alfred."

Markus's lips twitched. "Seth is an idiot."

Gwen shrugged, trying not to laugh at the teasing way Markus called his brother an idiot. "You know, now that I think of it, he does kind of look like Alfred from Batman."

The twitch of his lips turned into a slight smile. "Who, Seth? I'm sorry I don't see the likeness."

She laughed. "Look who has a sense of humor."

His smile disappeared and he turned away from her. She reached out to him, but didn't touch him. Uncertainty replaced the ease she started to feel around him. "Markus?"

"I've changed my mind about dinner. You don't have to dine with me. In fact, I think it would be best if we didn't."

Her gut tightened while her heart stuttered a couple of beats. She stared at his back for the longest, dumbfounded at the sudden shift in his mood. "You're joking, right?"

Turning to her, he narrowed eyes and set his mouth in a flat, straight line. "I don't joke."

And she didn't like his tone. "No, I guess you don't."

Turning on her heels, she walked toward the house.

It was foolish of her to think for a nanosecond that they could be friends or maybe more. Gods, she was stupid. Markus was not the boyfriend type. No, he was the type to take what he wanted then kick them to the curb.

All the signs were there. Hell, he even pushed her away until she insisted on him helping her. Yet she'd ignored the little voice, dismissed it as fear for her inner demons. Why? All because he'd said they were mates. What the hell did that mean for a dragon anyway?

Just as she reached for the door, Markus was there in a flash. Literally. He materialized in front of her, blocking the door.

"Move," she spat, too angry to look at him, and too afraid of what she'd see there.

With a finger, he reached out and caressed her cheek, then slid it under her chin. When he tried to make her look at him, she jerked her head to the side, breaking his hold. He let out a low growl that made her flinch a little, but she didn't cave. She couldn't give him the satisfaction of submitting to his demands.

Most of all, she couldn't let her fears rule her. It was time she grew a backbone and stood up to the monsters.

"Gwen, look at me."

Shaking her head, she took a step back. He flung his hand out, then curled it in to fist before he dropped it to his side. Softly, she said, "I want to go inside to eat my meal alone."

His jaw worked as if he was clenching his teeth or something. "You can eat out here."

"No, Markus, I can't."

"Why not?"

His harsh tone pissed her off. She stepped forward and jammed a finger into his chest. "Because you ruined it. The perfect evening, dinner under the stars with the sound of the ocean in the background. You ruined all of it. I thought that I'd actually started to like you, trust you enough to work with you. No, I can't work with you."

When she stepped around him, he let her go. Her chest tightened and she swallowed a lump in her throat as she opened the door and went straight to Markus's bedroom.

As expected, he followed her up the stairs. When she reached the room, she darted inside and closed and locked the door. Then she grabbed one of the blankets from the bed and a pillow and marched back to the door.

She opened it, threw the bedding at Markus's chest, and then slammed the door.

CHAPTER ELEVEN

Markus walked into his study and tossed the blanket and pillow on the sofa. *Damned woman.*

"Having female troubles?"

Markus jerked his gaze up toward the far corner of the study. Ares stood next to the floor to ceiling window, peering out. Movement to the left of him revealed Aphrodite sitting in an armchair with her legs draped over one arm.

It wasn't good when love *and* war came together to visit.

"What are you two doing here?"

Ares glanced over his shoulder, his dark brown eyes focused on Markus for several moments before he jerked his head to Aphrodite. "Ask her. This is her carnival ride."

Aphrodite rolled her eyes and swung her long legs

around so she sat straight in the chair. "Your father is grumpy because he knows I'm right."

Ares grunted from the window and shifted his gaze back out as if he was watching for something or someone. However, it was the goddess's words that sank in and made Markus study her closer. "Right about what?'

She looked at him and blinked. "Garrick needs to be stopped."

Markus's patience grew thin. The goddess's cryptic riddles gave him headaches, which he didn't need any more of right now. She'd always come to him with babbles of information in the form of short sentences and one word at a time conversations. It always ended the same way. Markus had to guess what she was trying to tell him and he'd have a headache when it was over.

Markus dropped down on the sofa and leaned his head against the back. "Aphrodite, I'm not in the mood for your games tonight."

"No games, Mark. We are all in trouble here whether Zeus wants to admit it or not."

Her tone was more serious than he'd ever heard it. Lifting his head, he looked into blue eyes identical to Gwen's. A hint of fear hid in the depths, making his blood warm and his dragon churn.

"What has happened?"

This time, Ares answered. "The veil between the Heavens and earth is thinning."

Shit. "How is that possible?"

Aphrodite looked at Ares, then to Markus. "We're

not sure. We have theories, but nothing to back them up. Zeus has released us from our bind that kept us from getting involved."

Markus narrowed his eyes and watched the two of them. "Who is 'our'? All the gods, or just you two?"

"Just us, but I fear others will start contacting their children soon."

Markus cursed and scrubbed a hand over his face. "We can't allow that to happen. Especially if their mortal children don't know a thing about them."

"That's what I said." Ares sat in Markus's chair behind his desk. He powered up the computer, then drew his brows together when the screen came on. It made Markus curious to what the hell could be on his computer screen. Sometimes Seth changed the background image to kittens or puppies.

Aphrodite stepped closer to him, drawing his attention. "The names on the list Gwen found are all first generation descendants."

Markus shifted his gaze to hers. "No, not all. Gwen is your granddaughter. Elle said she was a great-granddaughter of Nyx."

Frowning, she let her shoulders drop slightly. "Danielle is Nyx's daughter. Where is she?"

"Nyx?"

The goddess rolled her eyes. "No, Danielle."

Markus felt his lips lift. "She's in the basement hiding from Zavier."

Ares chuckled as he sat back in the chair and

propped his feet on the desk. Aphrodite crossed her arms over her chest. "What has your brother done to her?"

"You know as well as the rest of us that Zavier is the tamest of the group. Elle and Zavier are just avoiding each other. That's all."

Aphrodite smiled, wide. It made her angelic features look even more heavenly. In fact she seemed to glow from the inside. "They are soul mates." A bright smile formed on her face, and she strode toward the door, but Markus stopped her by grabbing her wrist.

"Do not interfere. You know we are cursed to death if we mate with a descendant."

She smiled again and patted him on the hand. "Yes, Zeus did say mate, but he never said anything about falling in love with your true soul mate."

Stunned, Markus stared at the goddess, waiting for her to say she was joking. All this time he'd been fighting the urge to claim Gwen as his. That was how he got stuck sleeping in the study. The realization that he was starting to care too much for the female made him think about how he couldn't have her without facing the death penalty. So he'd pushed her away, tried to deny his feelings despite believing she was his mate.

But could it really be as simple as true love?

"What are you not saying?" he demanded.

"It has to be true love between the both of you."

That explained a lot.

Before he could ask another question, she shook her

head. "Let your brothers know we are having a meeting and bring the women, too."

Ares raised a finger in the air. "Not Ashlynn."

Markus shifted his gazed from Ares to Aphrodite. "Why not?"

The goddess opened the study door and paused. "Because we're not sure whose side she's playing on. We'd rather keep her out of the loop for now."

GWEN STARED AT THE CEILING. Her pulse still raced. *Damned dragon. Why the hell did he have to be so complicated?* One minute he was charming, the next he withdrew behind his internal walls.

A light knock sounded on the door. Letting out a heavy sigh, she sat up and went to the door. "Who is it?"

"It's Elle."

Smiling, Gwen opened the door, grabbed her sister's hand and tugged her inside and hugged her. "Gods, I missed you."

Elle laughed. "It's only been a day." Pulling back out of the hug, she frowned. "What's wrong?"

Gwen shrugged. "Markus. The man drives me insane. Now that I'm not afraid of him, he's all I think about. It's crazy."

Laughing, Elle linked her fingers with Gwen's and pulled her toward the bed. They sat down facing one another. Gwen studied her sister. "You look tired."

One of Elle's shoulders raised in a shrug. "It's hard to sleep during the day and I'm too wound up at night to try."

"We have to tell them to keep it quiet so you can sleep."

Elle shook her head. "It's not the noise. It's Zavier. I can sense him when he's near. It's a little eerie. Do you know he watches me sleep?"

"That's creepy."

"As soon as he enters my studio in the basement, I wake up. He doesn't approach me, just watches."

Gwen hid her smile. Now that she thought about it, she'd noticed Markus watching her when he thought she wouldn't notice. Zavier could be taking an interest in Elle like Markus had Gwen.

"I wouldn't worry about it too much. I'll mention something to Markus about it."

Elle shrugged again. "Thanks. Hey, did you eat yet?"

Disappointment filled Gwen, making her think about Markus and his strange bi-polar personality at dinner. He seriously had to work on his mood swings. "No. Markus and I were supposed to have dinner, but he changed his mind."

"Just like that? What the hell is wrong with him?"

"I don't know. We were talking and he made a joke and when I said something about it, his mood changed. Maybe it's against the rules to make jokes or something."

Elle snickered. "It might be. They're immortal dragons. What do you expect?" She stood. "Come on, let's raid their huge-ass kitchen."

As soon as they turned to the door, it opened and Markus came in. "We're having a meeting downstairs."

Gwen narrowed her eyes, not moving for several moments. And she wouldn't have at all if Elle hadn't taken her by the arm and led her out of the bedroom and downstairs.

When they reached the foyer and turned to the great room, Gwen stilled, forcing Elle to stop. Good gods, it was Aphrodite. And Gwen assumed the man with her was Ares, but only because he looked so much like Markus. They weren't looking at her. The goddess had a hand on Ares's chest and his arm was around her waist as they whispered softly to each other.

Suddenly, Aphrodite turned her head and froze for a moment before pushing away from Ares and walked toward Gwen.

Taking an unsure step back, she wasn't sure what to expect. Sure, she'd seen photos of the goddess when she was little. Her dad kept them hidden in a desk drawer, but it was no surprise how much they looked alike.

Aphrodite stopped inches from her, tears filling her eyes. She lifted a hand as if to touch Gwen.

Shaking her head, Gwen extracted her arm from Elle's while still holding the goddess's gaze. "You let him die." The words were choked out and tears fell down her cheeks. "Why?"

Aphrodite closed her eyes briefly. "I had no choice. I…"

Gwen shook all over. Memories rose, bringing the pain of losing her parents stabbing her in the heart. She couldn't breathe.

Turning away from her grandmother, she rushed to the front door, opened it, and ran outside. She didn't stop until she reached the center of the rose gardens. Sitting on a stone bench, she covered her face with her hands and let the pain pour out of her.

After what felt like several minutes, she lifted her head and found Aphrodite waiting next to a yellow rose bush that was as tall as she was. "We were forbidden to have direct contact with our earth borne children. That didn't stop many of us from watching over them. Tom always seemed to know when I was near." The goddess let out a soft half-laugh, half-sob. "I admired his ambitions, his love for life." Aphrodite turned to face Gwen, and a tear rolled down her cheek. "After you were born, he summoned me and asked for my promise to keep you safe and, if I had to choose between him and you, that I must choose you."

Gwen sniffed and wiped her cheeks. "I don't understand. Why would he ask that of you?"

The goddess sighed and walked over to sit beside Gwen. "Your father had the gift of foresight. It was always hard for him to control, because he was half-human. I can only assume he saw something in your future, or his, or both."

Foresight? Gwen's father never mentioned this ability. Then again he never talked about any of his powers. The only time she'd witnessed that he had any was on one occasion—the night he died.

Glancing at her grandmother, Gwen studied her. There was so much she didn't know or understand about her life—the last few days had proven it. "The night my parents died…"

"Garrick came looking for you. When he didn't find you, he went for your parents."

Gwen's stomach twisted. "Why me?"

Aphrodite met her stare. "Because your mother was a minor goddess of fate. That is where you got your power of persuasion. It also makes you more powerful than any descendant that we know of."

"That's why you chose me?"

Aphrodite reached over and took her hand. "If I'd had a choice, I'd have chosen both of you. I loved Tom. The only thing I could do was cloak you from Garrick's sight."

"And keep Dad's promise."

Drawing her into a hug, Aphrodite pressed a kiss on her forehead and squeezed gently. "Yes. I'm so sorry."

Gwen didn't reply. Instead, she wrapped her arms around the goddess's waist and hugged her back. A connection she didn't know was missing snapped into place, filling the void in her soul. Aphrodite was her family.

"What about the direct contact thing?"

Her grandmother drew back, lifted Gwen's chin to meet her gaze, and smiled weakly. "It was lifted today, within reason." She rolled her eyes. "Or I should say within Zeus's reason, which can change at a moment's notice."

They fell silent for a few moments, then Gwen said, "I guess we should get back inside."

Aphrodite released her and stood. "Come, we have much to plan if we're going to save the worlds."

CHAPTER TWELVE

Markus sensed Gwen's and Aphrodite's presences the moment they entered the house. A few seconds later, they walked into the great room. Gwen met his eyes briefly and sat on the sofa next to Elle. His dragon roared in his head and nudged him to go to her. The need to be near her intensified every time he saw and smelled her.

Now that he knew he could have her, it was going to be impossible to stay away. Why should he? If she was his true mate and chose to be with him, Zeus couldn't stop them.

Aphrodite's words still rang in his ears.

...Zeus did say mate, but he never said anything about falling in love with your true soul mate.

Shaking off the thought, he scanned around the room and met Ares's glare from across the room where he leaned against the wall, arms crossed. *You first, father.*

Ares smirked at the telepathic contact and spoke to the group. "Garrick is pissing me off."

Seth snorted. "Yeah? Well, join the club."

Aphrodite passed by him and sent the god a narrowed-eyed glare as she came to stand in the center of the sitting area. "The names on the list are all very powerful descendants. We know Gwen is my grand-daughter, but she is also the granddaughter of one of the Fates. I'm not sure which one and they won't answer any of my calls."

Turning her attention to Elle, she smiled. "Danielle, Nyx is not your great-grandmother. She is your mother. Your full powers mirror that of Death's. You can pass between earth and the Underworld."

Elle shook her head. Gwen took her hand in hers. "But my dad said…"

Aphrodite held up a hand, stopping Elle. "Your parents were protecting you. Your own knowledge of your legacy could be turned against you. The mother who raised you couldn't have children of her own. Nyx gifted her with a child."

"I don't understand."

"The Goddess of Night is an elemental god. She can't take a physical form for long periods of time."

Elle sat back into the couch and sighed. "Are you saying that Nyx bargained with my mother to sleep with my dad? I'm not buying that. My parents were too much in love."

Aphrodite rolled her neck, as if tired. "In a way. Nyx bargained to be a part of the act. She joined Jessica's soul as she made love to your father. In exchange, Jessica got you."

Elle still shook her head. Markus expected her to leave the room, but she just sat on the sofa, hand-in-hand with Gwen. Her drawn brows and pursed lips told him that Elle was having a hard time processing the information.

Ares cleared his throat impatiently before he spoke. "The other women on the list are also first generation, but none of them know it."

Drake broke his silence beside Markus. "You don't happen to know where they are, do you?"

Ares straightened and unfolded his arms. "Nope. That's your job."

Drake held up his middle finger while he took a swig of his beer.

Ty shifted in his chair next to the sofa. "Any hints? Are they in this country at least?"

Ares shrugged, but it was Aphrodite who answered. "All we know is that Rayna is on the west coast. Faith is on the east. Their divine mothers are hiding them."

"And who are their mothers?" Markus asked.

"Rayna's is Themis, goddess of divine law. Faith's mother is Nike, goddess of victory"

Markus nearly chocked on his beer. The descendants

of Law and Victory could never fall into Garrick's control. With a goddess of law, he could challenge Themis and, if he succeeded in killing her, rewrite the divine laws. With the power that Faith held, Garrick could increase the amount of wars among the humans.

He met Gwen's gaze. "Can you let me know if you find out anything in your father's journals?"

"Of course."

Drake stood. "I'll see if I can get any hits on the names. Aphrodite, do you know their ages? Or their birthdays? That would help narrow the search."

The goddess shook her head. "I can try to find out. I'm also going to talk to Themis and Nike and see if they'll give me anything. I can't make promises, but I'll try."

Zavier rose from where he sat behind the bar, a tablet in his hand. "I'll help Drake with computer searches." Walking around the bar, he moved toward Gwen. Markus didn't miss the way Elle tensed when Zavier reached between them from behind the sofa and handed Gwen the tablet. "All the journal files are loaded as well as some research notes I found."

She took the hand held computer. "Thank you."

A few moments later, Markus was alone with Gwen, surprised she stayed behind when the others left. He remained silent while he drank the last of his beer, unsure of what to say to her. The knowledge of them being mates didn't sit well her. That led him to think she wouldn't believe him if he told her they were fated to be together.

The silence finally got to him and he set the beer bottle down hard enough the sound echoed through the downstairs. Gwen flinched, but didn't look at him.

"I don't understand the things I feel when I'm around you."

There. He said it.

Studying her hands in her lap, she sagged into the sofa. "I'm starting to care for you more than I should. It scares me."

MARKUS'S SHADOW fell across Gwen as he stopped in front of her. She glanced up and he held out his hand. Reluctantly, she placed her hand in his and allowed him to pull her to her feet. With their fingers linked, he tugged her toward the kitchen. "What are you doing?"

"I'm making you something to eat, since I ruined dinner."

Guilt crept up her spine. "Look, Markus, earlier I was tired and sore and frustrated. I didn't…"

He stopped and turned around. "Don't apologize. I was an ass. I'm always an ass. Just ask my brothers."

One corner of his lips lifted, making her smile. "Okay, but I was being crabby as well."

Closing the distance, he lowered his head and kissed her lightly. Moaning, she leaned into him, but he ended the kiss much too soon. With a raised brow, he turned around and led her to the kitchen.

Markus set her on the counter beside him as he chopped vegetables for an omelet. He'd said it was the only thing he knew how to make. The confession made her laugh and her heart melted a little more.

When she turned on the tablet Zavier gave her, she noticed the files were neatly placed in a folder with her father's name. Opening the folder she scanned over the journal entries while asking Markus questions.

"Do you think I'll find something useful in my father's journals?"

He shrugged. "I hope so. Even if it's only a small amount of information, it's more than we know now."

Good point. If her dad worked with Garrick, then there was bound to be something he recorded. "What if Dad didn't know anything?"

As soon as she asked the question she knew the answer. "Never mind. Aphrodite said my father had foresight. She said it was unpredictable, but I'm guessing he could have seen something."

Markus nodded. "Let's hope he did."

"Can I ask a personal question?

"Sure."

"You didn't have a childhood, right?"

He paused chopping for brief moment, then resumed. "No. Have you heard the legend of the Spartoi?"

When she nodded, he continued. "We are the Spartoi, or the Sons of War. Although the truth has been modified over the centuries. After Ares's dragon was slain in a battle between the gods and their earth borne children, Ares sowed one set of the dragon's teeth into the earth. From the teeth were born the Spartoi."

"How many of you were there?"

"Hundreds, I believe." Turning to her, he took her hand. "We were very different back then. When we rose from the earth, all we knew was what Ares commanded."

She squeezed his hand, brought it to her mouth and pressed a kiss in his palm. "I understand. I've studied the history of the gods and heard stories from my father. Go on."

His lips lifted in a sensual smile and his shoulders relaxed. "We fought alongside the gods and won the war. The descendants were sent back to earth with no memories of their ancestry, and their powers were bound."

"How long did you live in Olympus before you were banished?"

He shrugged. "A few centuries."

Moving to stand in front of her, he took the tablet out of her hand and set it on the counter. Before he had a chance to remove her from where she sat, she wrapped her legs around his waist and tugged him closer.

The corner of lips twitched. "Are you looking for trouble?"

She smiled. "I found trouble a long time ago and can't get rid of it."

A chuckle left his lips and he leaned in and kissed her long and hard as if knowing exactly what she wanted. She slipped her tongue into his mouth. His hands tightened on her hip, not too tight, but tight enough it sent a jolt of excitement and desire rushing through her veins.

Breaking the kiss, Markus rested his forehead against hers. "You need to eat before it gets cold."

Defeated, she released him and allowed him to lift her off the counter and led her to his study.

Thirty minutes later, Gwen was curled up on the sofa with the pillow she threw at Markus earlier under her head and the blanket draped over her as she read one of her father's journal entries.

September 8, 1976

I met the most interesting man today at University. I was going over my civics papers in the student courtyard when he approached me to ask for directions to the main office. At first I thought he was a new student who'd gotten lost, as many freshmen did in the first few weeks of the semester. So, I gave him directions.

That was when he noticed the stack of papers in front of me. He asked if I was a teacher, then went on about how he'd studied Greek mythology his whole life. Since I didn't have any more classes, I introduced myself and offered him a seat.

He accepted with a smile and said his name was

Garrick.

We talked for hours about the theories and mysteries of the gods and which were our favorites and least favorites. I was so intrigued to have someone who shared my passion for research, I agreed to have coffee with him tomorrow.

Gwen looked up from the tablet and to Markus, who was clicking away at his keyboard. "What are you doing?"

He glanced at her and his expression softened a little. "Making schedules for the staff for the next week. Then I'm going to research a few names Drake sent me."

"Oh."

"Why? What do you need?"

She shook her head. "Nothing. Just curious."

Motioning to the tablet, he asked, "How's reading going?"

"Garrick and my father met at the university he taught at before I was born."

"What was Garrick doing there?"

"I'm not sure. Dad didn't say. Only that a man approached him in the student courtyard and they started talking." She read the passage to him.

Markus sat back in his chair and stared at her for a few moments. "Now I'm curious. My brother must had known Tom was a descendant and sought him out."

Gwen glanced back at the tablet and scrolled through the entries, skimming them for Garrick's name or anything that stuck out. Markus knelt in front of her a moment later and took the tablet.

"You're tired and it's late."

Yawning, she shook her head. "I'm not tired."

He cocked an eyebrow and she laughed. "Okay, maybe a little."

"I'm taking you to bed." Wrapping the blanket around her, he scooped her up.

She didn't fight him, didn't have the energy. "Markus?"

"Hmm."

"Are you coming to bed, too?"

As if the question surprised him, he stopped with one foot on the first step. "Only if you promise to go to sleep."

Smiling, she rested her head against his chest. "Deal."

GARRICK PACED his large bedroom suite as his patience evaporated. Ashlynn had left two days before and he still hadn't heard from her. Her cell was off and he couldn't track her through his bond with her. The witch must have broken it without his knowledge.

The mystery was how had she done it.

He picked up the glass on the table beside him and threw it at the door. Crystal splintered into pieces and scattered over the floor. A knock sounded.

"Come in."

Slowly, the door opened and a male descendant peeked his head inside, his eyes wide and unsure. *As he should be.*

"Don't make me say it again."

The male rushed inside, shut the door, and leaned against it. "I have word about Ash."

Garrick growled. The damned female insisted on being called by that nickname. It drove him insane. Then again, that was why she did it, to push his buttons.

"Go on," Garrick prompted.

"She killed the group of scouts you sent to follow her. Well, all but one, who only lived long enough to make it back and tell me." The descendant, Joel, was only twenty-one and one of the most powerful demi-gods, besides Ash, Garrick currently had in his possession. That didn't mean he was the smartest.

"Joel," Garrick growled in warning.

"Craig said that Ash was injured in the process, and after she killed the others and sent him back here, she headed up the mountain in the direction we believe the dragons live."

Fuck. He was afraid she'd one day betray him, but he'd figured it'd be after he unlocked the gates between earth and the Heavens.

Now it seemed Ashlynn had plans of her own. He'd just have to make sure she went down with his brothers. *In ashes.*

CHAPTER THIRTEEN

Ash stepped out of the bedroom and peeked down the hall. The house was quiet and she wondered where the dragons were. Surprisingly, they didn't have a guard outside her door. Then again, they could have the whole house under surveillance.

With slow, steady steps, she crept down the hallway and froze as a door somewhere behind her opened. *Shit*. Bracing herself for a confrontation with one of the dragons, she turned slowly. Relief rolled over her at the sight of Thea pulling a door shut with one hand and a load of towels in the other.

The dark haired nymph spotted her and smiled. "Hello, miss. It is good to see you up."

Ash placed a finger over her lips. "Shh." She rushed over to take the towels from her, but Thea waved her off.

"Don't shush me. Besides it does no good to try to

sneak around the mansion. There are five dragons in this house." The nymph laughed as she walked down the hall to a laundry chute in the corner. Tossing the linen down it, she turned to head back toward her.

Ash frowned. Thea had a point. "Why are you here, working as their maid?"

Thea shook her head and opened another door. "I don't do anything here I didn't do for Aphrodite."

The nymph disappeared inside the room. Ash poked her head in and noticed it was an occupied room—a dragon's room. It smelled of man and dark, sweet spice. Her skin prickled, making her shudder.

"Whose room is this?"

"Ty's and don't come in. He doesn't like females." Thea came out of the bathroom with a roll of soiled towels.

Ash drew back. "What do you mean? Is he gay?"

"No. How to say it right?" She thought about it for a moment. "He doesn't trust them and doesn't like them near him or his stuff."

Odd. "Why?"

"Don't know. Even if I did, I wouldn't tell you."

"Why not?"

"Because it's none of your business."

Ash rolled her eyes and stepped away from the doorway so Thea could exit. "What about you?"

"He tolerates me and Ariel inside, but we are to only touch the linen. He does his own cleaning."

Ash peeked inside the room again and had to admit

it was clean. Much cleaner than her room in the village or Garrick's rooms at the compound. A shiver ran down her spine at the thought of Garrick.

Yeah, he was going to be pissed at her betrayal. The cherry topping would come when he found out where she was and what her true mission was. A smile tugged at her lips. When she met Thea's stare, Ash's smile widened.

Thea folded her arms over her chest. "What are you thinking? Because if you're thinking of hurting them in any way…"

Thea's tone changed from sweet to vicious in a blink. Ash reached out and touched her arm. "Calm down. I'm not plotting to harm any of them." Not physically, anyway. She might break a heart, but all was fair in war.

Thea's defensive and protective tone made Ash curious. "Do they treat you well?"

The nymph wrinkled her nose. "Of course, goddess."

Ash rushed forward and place a finger on Thea's lips. "You mustn't call me that."

Thea pushed her hand away and tsked. "It is what you are. Besides, the sons are not the monsters Garrick would like you to believe."

Ash raised a brow. "What do you know?"

A sheepish smile formed. "Aphrodite visits often and shares all the secrets with us so that we can assist the sons when needed."

Unbelievable. Aphrodite seemed to have her hand in this war more than she or Artemis guessed. Setting up her chess pieces to aid the precious dragons she was so fond of. "What about Ares?"

Thea shrugged and carried the towels to the chute. "He pops in from time to time, but I think it is more to annoy Markus. War makes me uneasy, so I stay away from him." She opened a linen closet next to the chute and took out a couple of towels and a wash cloth. After placing the towels in the room, she came back out and said, "I must go. It's my turn to help the chef with the meal."

"Okay, but promise we can have tea and talk some more?"

Thea's face brightened. "I'd love that. I'll tell Ariel, too."

The nymph turned toward the stairs, waving as she went.

Ash's body stiffened as the scent of male and sweet spice intensified, followed by a dark power she knew as that of the dragons. Her skin tightened and warmed all at once. The heat of his body kissed her flesh in a sensual tease that ignited both desire and fear.

"I hope you didn't taint my room with your scent, female."

Ash held in her moan and closed her eyes. "What if I did, dragon?"

A low growl rumbled at her back. "I'd be forced to

hunt you down." He leaned in to whisper, his lips barely brushing her ear. "And fuck you until you screamed."

Well, damn.

Unsure if he intended that to be a threat or a promise, she was tempted to go into the room and mark every inch of it.

Turning around, slowly, she gasped at the pure masculine beauty of him. Tyson was perfection of the male form, except for a white cluster of scars that peeked from under the right side of the sunglasses he always wore. To her, the scars only added to his appeal. From the multiple times she'd spied on him over the centuries, she knew that hard muscles covered his body.

He inhaled deeply and one side of his kissable mouth curled. "You'd like that, wouldn't you, goddess?"

"I'm no goddess." By the way his dark brow rose above the rim of the shades, he knew she lied.

He flattened her against the wall faster than she could blink, his hard body pressed into her, confining her. Lifting her chin, she tried like hell to tamp down the desire rushing through her. Everywhere he touched her burned and damn if she didn't want more.

"Your powers are not bound. I can smell them. I can smell that bastard of a brother of mine on you as well."

Fear burned in her belly, but before she could respond he stepped back a few feet, leaving her to sag against the wall. Then he was gone.

Heart hammering, she glanced around and met the concerned stare of one of the women Garrick was searching for. The same one Ash saw Markus carry from the lighthouse the day before.

"Hello, I'm Gwen." She held out her hand. When Ash didn't take it, the other woman frowned. "Are you okay?"

Ash straightened and smoothed her top. "I'm fine." Turning, she started to walk off when Gwen spoke again.

"I came to check on you, but since you're awake, would you like to go to the market with me?"

Turning back around, Ash studied her for a moment. "Are you going alone?"

Gwen shook her head. "Seth is coming."

Ash almost said no, but figured she could use the time to see what Gwen knew about the dragons. Also, Ash was curious about the female's powers. Garrick had always said she was powerful, or would be once she was unleashed, yet, he never said exactly what they were.

"Sure. I'll come with you."

Gwen smiled. "Great. Meet us in the foyer in five minutes?"

The petite blond demi-goddess whirled around and rushed down the hall, then disappeared inside a room.

Only once she was alone did Ash allow a satisfied smile spread across her face. Artemis was right. This was more exciting than hanging out with Garrick and waiting for the idiot to make a move.

Besides, Ash knew which of the brothers she was going to seduce.

"How did you come into you powers?" Gwen asked as she picked up a tomato from the vegetable stand. Ash stilled for a brief moment before replying.

"I'm not sure really. I was kidnapped several years ago by a crazy dragon shifter that I learned later was one of the Sons of War."

It was Gwen's turn to still her motions. Turning to the other woman, Gwen studied her. "You mean Garrick?"

Nodding, Ash lowered her voice as if trying to keep Seth, who leaned against the front counter a few feet away flirting with the cashier, from hearing their conversation. "He gave me an injection of something that unlocked my powers."

"How did you get away?" Gwen tried to keep the suspicion out of her voice. There was something in the way Ash spoke, or maybe it was her tone, that rang Gwen's internal warning bells. The other woman wasn't being a hundred percent honest.

Ash picked up a few mangos and added them to the basket. "I killed my guards and the three scouts that were sent after me."

Gwen jerked her gaze over to meet Ash's. "Wow. You say that like it was nothing."

"The descendants he has under him aren't all there. I don't know how to explain it. It's just like they are under some kind of trance or their humanity has been wiped from them."

Again Gwen picked up on a half-truth. Her palms itched to reach out to touch Ash and "persuade" her to tell her everything. No, Gwen had promised to never use her gift for negative or selfish purposes. "What about you? You said guards. Did he keep you locked up?"

Glancing over at Seth, who had moved away from the counter and now sat at a table a few feet away at a small café, Ash whispered, "Garrick kept me on a short leash for his own pleasures."

Gwen was about to ask another question, but Ash touched her arm and looked into her eyes. At first, fear that Ash had a similar gift flooded her senses, but Gwen didn't feel any magic or excess power coming from the other woman. Relaxing, Gwen held Ash's stare as she whispered, "You must not speak of my captivity to the dragons. I don't want them to think I'm working with Garrick."

Narrowing her eyes, Gwen asked with a little too much protectiveness for the five men who'd saved her and Elle's life, "Why did you come to their home?"

"I was hoping they'd help me hide for a while, until I can contact my mother."

There. Gwen had the little tidbit she needed to dig deeper, because she knew Artemis was Ash's mother. Thea had told them that when Ash first arrived at the house.

Before she had a chance to ask her next question,

Ash grabbed her hand and yelled, "Seth, heads up." She pulled Gwen down the street, then started to run. Gwen stumbled a few steps before falling into a run with Ash. Her heat hammered in her ears.

Dark magic coated her senses in thick waves. Gwen's skin felt like a millions tiny insects were crawling all over. "What the hell is that?"

"You really don't want to know." Ash turned left, forcing Gwen to follow.

They ran down an empty side street with whatever the hell it was chasing them. Gwen didn't dare look back. "Where are we going?"

Ash twisted around to glance behind them. "The beach. There's no humans there this time of year. I hope."

Yeah, so did Gwen.

Suddenly a sharp pain shot up her leg and she screamed as she fell to the ground. Ash was there instantly, bent over her checking the wound on her calf. Blood soaked her jeans. Meeting Ash's gaze, Gwen shook her head. "Tell me you have a plan."

A roar echoed off the building around them, making Gwen's heart beat at an incredible rate. They turned at the same time toward the sound and Gwen gasped. "Holy shit. Is that a...?"

"A cyclops, yes."

Blocking Gwen from view of the one-eyed giant, Ash fell into a protective stance. A moment later a bow and arrow appeared in her hand. Gwen wasn't sure if she should be in awe of Ash's powers or frightened. Relief sparked inside her and she was glad the other woman was on her side, for now.

Ash shouldered a quiver, pulled an arrow out, and positioned it. She drew back the bow and released it, sending the arrow hurling in the air and into the creature's shoulder. But nothing happened. The beast didn't even flinch.

Cursing, Ash fired another arrow, but the bow was knocked out of her hand by a man who materialized next to them. He grabbed Ash, twisted her around so her back pressed against his front, and held a knife to her throat.

Gwen met Ash's gaze, then kicked out with her good leg, hitting the man in the shin. Cursing, he reached down and grabbed Gwen by the arm.

It was exactly the outcome she hoped for. Although, she needed skin-to-skin contact for her gift to work. She got the opportunity when he released her briefly and wrapped his arm around her waist. Grabbing onto the exposed section of forearm, Gwen released her hold on the little power she had and whispered, "Let us go, then drive the knife into your own heart."

Ash's eyes grew huge as if she figured out what Gwen had done. Yeah, so her secret was out. The only thing to do now was pray to the gods that Ash didn't betray them.

The man did exactly what Gwen told him. Shock

and confusion whirled over his features as he plunged the dagger deep into his chest and fell to the ground.

A moment later a loud crash sounded behind her and the ground shook under her feet. Turning, Gwen saw the cyclops face down on the pavement. Ash glanced at Gwen and gave her a satisfied smirk.

"Good thinking on the persuasion thing."

Gwen nodded, she shook so bad she wasn't sure how much longer she could hold it together. Dragons were one thing, but one-eyed, man-eating giants were another.

The air around her energized like an electronic charge went off. She twisted around, ready to take on whatever the hell it was. Relief washed through her as she looked into Markus's midnight blue eyes.

When he reached out to her, she jumped at him, wrapping her arms around his waist and squeezing. "Where's Seth?" Fear crept in at the idea of the cyclops killing Seth.

"He's fine. He and Ty are leading another cyclops out of town." Markus paused, making Gwen look up to see him glare at Ash. "You have a lot of explaining to do."

Ash nodded. "I know. Let's get her back to the mansion. I'll explain when everyone gets there."

Markus gripped Ash by the upper arm and tele-ported them back to the house.

CHAPTER FOURTEEN

Markus materialized inside the foyer with Gwen and Ashlynn. His blood boiled at the fact that Gwen had gotten hurt. He'd smelled her blood the moment he took form beside them in the village.

Releasing Ashlynn, he motioned to the great room. "Have a seat."

She rolled her eyes, but obeyed. *Smart female.*

Carrying Gwen to the sofa, he sat her down gently, then ripped the leg of her jeans from the bottom up to her knee. "Thea!"

The dark haired nymph appeared in the archway between the rooms. When she saw Gwen, she rushed forward and shooed Markus out of the way while she worked to heal her wound.

"Do you know what caused this?" Markus asked no one in particular, but Thea answered.

"A god bolt."

His blood went cold while his temper heated. "When in Hades did cyclopes start using god bolts?"

Ash clicked her tongue against the roof of her mouth. "They don't. They're not smart enough."

The front door blew open and Ty and Seth stormed in, their dragons still in their eyes. At least Seth's was. Markus knew by the way Ty strode across the room that his was very close to the surface.

"Stupid ass giants weren't alone. There was a demi-god with them." Seth walked past Ty to stop in front of Gwen, a frown on his face.

Gwen glanced up and drew her brows together. "This is not your fault."

Thea stood and addressed Gwen. "Can I get you anything else?"

"No. Thanks."

Markus nodded his thanks to Thea and she left. Glancing back at Ash, he didn't bother to keep the annoyance out of his voice. "Someone needs to start talking."

Ty dropped into the armchair opposite Ashlynn. "Where are Drake and Z?"

Drake walked in with a beer in one hand and a sandwich in the other. "Z is on his way. He went to get Elle."

Seth let out a sigh and sat on the couch next to Gwen. "I didn't sense the cyclopes. I didn't even see them until Ash yelled my name."

Markus turned to the redheaded goddess. "Why don't you share how you knew they were there?"

Ash drummed her fingers on the chair arm. "I'm Artemis's daughter and I was born on Olympus."

"Tells us something we don't know, goddess." Ty grinned and leaned forward in his seat.

Mimicking his movement, Ash raised a brow in challenge. "I'm a spy for the gods."

Ty started to stand, but stopped when Markus held up a hand. "Ashlynn, we don't have time for games."

"She's telling the truth," Gwen said as she stared at the other woman. "I knew there was something you were leaving out when we talked in the village."

Markus studied Gwen. "Are you sure?"

Gwen nodded. "I'm not sure how I know. I just do. I've always been able to tell if someone was being truthful with me or not."

A short laugh burst from Ashlynn, drawing his attention to her. "A daughter of the Fates. Of course. That's why Garrick is so hard up to have her."

Stepping between the females, Markus growled, "What do you know about Garrick?"

Ashlynn sat back in the chair and picked at the edge of the arm. "I've spent the last two years with him, working with him. I know his routines, but he never fully trusted me to share the details."

Zavier and Elle came into the room. Elle saw Gwen and rushed over to take the empty seat next to her. When she did, Gwen leaned into her. "I'm fine."

"And we have Night." Ashlynn laughed.

Ty growled. Markus cut a glance at his brother.

"Silence." Then he turned back to Ashlynn. "Go on. Speak your mind."

"With Nyx's daughter under his control, Garrick could control most of the night crawlers and some Underworld demons. With Gwen, I'm guessing he could use her gift of persuasion and unlock her full powers to change the fate of everyone around him." Ashlynn stood and began to pace. "But that would only be the start. Diversions for the grand master plan. Damn, I should have stuck around longer."

Gwen shook her head. "He would have grown more suspicious. What if he isn't sure about his own plan?"

Markus meet Gwen's gaze. "What do you mean?"

"Like if he had several different plans. Like, backups in case…"

"In case something went wrong." Ashlynn snapped her fingers then pointed at Gwen. "You're right. Come to think of it, he had scouts out looking for you and Elle because you were always together. Meanwhile, he has two more groups out looking for two other descendants."

Markus asked, even though he knew the answer. "What are their names?"

"Rayna and Faith. I'm not sure of their last names. I only know that much because I saw the names in his notes." Ashlynn sat back down on the chair and dropped her shoulders. "I failed. The whole mission. I didn't learn a damn thing about his plan to bring war against the gods."

Drake broke his silence. "Why did you leave and how?"

"I wanted to see which side of the war you're playing for." She lifted her gaze to look at Ty. "Plus, I got tired of being his personal outlet when something went wrong."

Markus saw Ty's hands ball up into fists as if trying to control his dragon. The subject of Garrick, his betrayal to them and the gods, and his grand plan to take over the Heavens always raised the tension in the mansion.

"So how did you leave?"

"I told him I would track down Gwen myself."

Markus took a step toward her, but Seth stood and placed a hand on his shoulder. "We all have to calm down. Don't forget, she saved Gwen's life today. She could have let the cyclops take them."

Ashlynn shrugged. "It was Gwen who saved us both. She 'persuaded' the descendant to kill himself instead of me."

Gwen ducked her head. "Yeah, but you shot the arrow into the beast's eye."

Markus glanced from one female to the other and realized that they'd formed a silent alliance. He, on the other hand, wasn't so sure Artemis's daughter could be trusted just yet. "Ashlynn, what else can you tell us about Garrick?"

"Desperation is setting in. I could only imagine the kind of tantrum he's throwing right now."

Seth snorted. "Ty sent the descendant who was meant as my distraction back to Gary with the cyclops's ear."

Ashlynn pressed her lips together as if hiding a smile. "Well, if that doesn't successfully piss him off, I have a better way."

Markus studied her for a moment before asking, "What would that be?"

She hesitated. "Garrick mentioned once that he believed his mate was still alive."

Warning bells sounded off in Markus's mind, but it was Ty who spoke. "Why would he tell you something that personal?"

Ashlynn's gaze locked with Ty's, and for a moment Markus thought he'd have command his brother to leave the room. However, she dropped her shoulders and sat back in the chair. "My orders were to get as close to him as I could."

Ty let out a low growl and Markus swung his head around. *What the fuck is wrong with you?* He thought to his brother.

Meeting his gaze, Ty stood and stared for a few moments before he turned and left the room. Markus blew out a breath and scrubbed a hand over his face. "How much information do you have about Garrick?"

Ash shrugged. "Not much more than you, really. He'd ramble about things when we were alone, saying things like my hair reminded him of hers. Also, he was set up for her death and that was why he seeks revenge on the gods."

Seth grunted. "I bet his vengeance against us is because we're trying to stop him."

"That and he believes Ty killed her."

Drake set his beer on the bar countertop, hard. "The fuck he did. They were mated. He knew none of us would hurt his mate."

Gwen shifted slowly on the sofa next to where Markus stood. "So why does he believe she's still alive?"

Markus answered. "Because he's mad. We all saw the body and we were all there when Zeus came in and issued his curse, banning us from the Heavens."

Ashlynn sighed. "I asked my mother the same question. She said that when a dragon loses a mate, sometimes they go insane."

Out of reflex, Markus glanced at Gwen, who stared back at him as if she knew his train of thought. Shaking his head, he turned away from the group.

Ashlynn cleared her throat. "We should keep a watch on all the elements. I wouldn't put it past him to conjure up a natural disaster or something."

Markus nodded, but his mind was on others things. Things like mating and Gwen. When he turned back to her, he let out a soft growl as he caught her sneaking out of the living room.

Without another word, he set his jaw and followed her, leaving everyone else behind. As far as he was concerned, the meeting was over. There was nothing they could do at the moment, but wait. Markus on the other hand was going to stalk his mate down and have the conversation she'd tried to avoid.

GWEN ENTERED the bedroom she shared with Markus and sat down on the bed. Gods, she was tired. It was like all the energy had been drained from her. Maybe it had something to do with the amount of power it took to bend the will of the man who held Ash at knifepoint.

She curled up on the bed and closed her eyes, her whole body relaxing against the soft comforter. A moment later she heard the door open, then close with a soft click. Markus's earthy scent filled the room in a soft and soothing wave.

"Gwen?"

The concern in his hushed tone made her open her eyes and meet his gaze. "I'm fine, just tired."

Her eyes drifted shut again, finding it hard to keep them open. Never had she been so tired before. Rustling of clothes made her open her eyes to see Markus taking his shoes off, then his shirt, revealing a naturally tanned chest and washboard abs. A surge of energy shot through her as her mouth went dry and she had the strange urge to kiss every inch of his exposed skin.

Easing down on the bed beside her, he rested his back

against the headboard, then gathered her in his arms. Almost instantly her muscles relaxed. When she cuddled into him and rested her head on his warm chest, a sense of belonging filled her. Like they belonged together.

He kissed the top of her head. "Tell me about what happened in the village."

Her brows bunched together. "What do you mean? Ash already told you and the others what happened."

Absently he rubbed her back in soothing, circular motions. "I want to hear it from you."

The spark of energy was gone and she was now annoyed and tired. "You don't trust her."

"Why should I?"

"Like I said earlier, I can sense a lie. I asked her questions while we were shopping around and before we were attacked. Although at the time she didn't tell me the whole truth, she didn't lie to me either."

"You questioned her?"

There was a smile in his voice and it made her relax further. "Yes. I learned pretty much what she revealed to everyone here without so much detail. I don't think she is here to do harm."

"Why do you think she is here?"

"Because she's curious about you and your brothers. I think she's been told terrible things about the Sons of War and wants to know the truth for herself."

Markus grunted and shifted as if getting comfortable. "Maybe. I don't think she's playing on our side.

She's a hunter sent down from the gods. For what, I'm not sure."

"Could be for insurance, like she's to stop the war before it begins, no matter what the cost."

With his index finger, he lifted her chin so she met his gaze. "How do you know?"

Gwen smiled. "I studied the myths alongside my father for as long as I can remember. Plus, my ability to decipher lies allows me to weed out the false myths or the half-truths written in many literatures to keep humans from the truth of the Heavens and the gods."

He smiled, but there was a hint of worry she was sure he tried to hide from her. "Garrick would use your gifts to break the barriers between the Heavens and the earth."

"I know." She laid her head back on his chest.

"What happened when you killed the Imperial?"

A sick feeling churned in her belly. "It was self-defense."

Drawing her closer, he kissed her forehead. "You did what you had to. Plus, he would have killed you without a thought."

He was right. The hatred in the man's features as he held Ash at knifepoint said there was no pure bone left in his body. "I felt helpless while Ash was being threatened. I did the only thing I knew I could. As soon as I got in the position to make skin contact with him, I poured everything into him and told him to let us go and stab his own heart."

Relief flooded her when Markus didn't move away. Instead he continued the slow, calming circles on her back with his fingers. "That's why you are tired. Well, that and your body is healing itself."

Nodding, she yawned and let her eyes drift close. She'd guessed the same thing. The ability to heal three times faster than a normal human had always made her a little low on energy. With the extent of the injury from the god bolt and the amount of power she used on the Imperial male, she wasn't surprised she was so tired.

Even with Thea's help healing.

"Sleep. You'll need your strength for training tomorrow."

A smiled tugged at her lips. "I'll kick your butt all over the gym this time."

He chuckled and eased down so he laid flat on the mattress. "That sounds like a challenge, Ms. Preston."

"You betcha..." she said as she drifted off to sleep.

CHAPTER FIFTEEN

June 29, 1977

It's been about nine months since I met my friend, Garrick, and about six months since I started working in his research division. The amount of reference material that I have at my disposal is overwhelming and exciting. I wish I could call on my mother to verify the authenticity of it all. Then again, if she was permitted to talk with me, I could ask her directly what I desired to know. Like, how many others like me are out there? I know there are others. I just haven't found them.

Yet, Aphrodite is bound by the curse placed on them all by Zeus after the war between the gods and humans thousands of years ago. She, like all the other gods, is not allowed direct contact with her earth borne children.

I understand the whys, but I don't understand the

logic. My powers are bound. I'm no threat to the gods, nor do I have any desire to overtake the Heavens.

I want to keep the balance between the worlds and find others like me to help keep that balance. That's what I'm hoping Garrick will be able to help me with and the reason why I told him about my heritage today. I was pleased to learn that he, too, is a demi-god. He shares my vision of meeting others like us.

He even told me he's working on a way to unlock our powers to aid in finding the others. I'm excited to finally be able to give back to the gods who watch over us.

Gwen stopped reading and glanced around the too quiet room. She, Markus, and Zavier came to the study after she'd showed Markus the journal entry. "It's not much, but it's a start, right?"

Markus nodded, but it was Zavier who spat out, "Gary is no more a demi-god than I can transform into Pegasus."

Gwen laughed, but pressed her lips together when she met Markus's unamused gaze. His mouth was set in a harsh line. Amused, she bit back a giggle, because his lips twitched as if withholding his smile. It was in the way his eyes shimmered from the black of the dragon to the dark blue that was his natural eye color.

"My father always had a good, caring heart. He saw the positive in everything." A lump formed in her throat and she swallowed it, not allowing the pain to rise and overtake her. It was time to move past the pain and seek the justice that would make Tom Preston proud.

Zavier sat next to her. "You mentioned research division. That almost confirms my theory that Garrick has a home base somewhere."

"He has to sleep somewhere," Gwen said.

Markus tapped his finger on the dark, cherry-colored oak desk. "Not necessarily. We don't need a lot of sleep. Maybe a few hours a day. Sometimes, if needed, we can go for days without sleep."

Gwen thought about that. "Well, hell. That would mean he could be anywhere while his Imperials are managing home base."

Zavier nodded. "But it's just as important that we find the facilities and take them out."

"Ash will know."

Markus snorted. "And she'd tell us, why?"

Gwen narrowed her gaze at him. "Because I'm going to ask her."

The dragon on the other side of desk held her gaze for several moments before raising his brow. "Give all the info to Zavier, even if it is a half-truth or untrue. Gods have a way of twisting words so they can tell you things without coming out and saying them."

"Ash isn't a goddess."

Markus sighed. "Yes, she is a goddess by law. She was born in Olympus."

And because Gwen was born on earth, and had her

powers locked at birth, she wasn't worthy of the title. Even though she was only one third human.

Whatever, she wasn't sure she wanted to be a goddess anyway. Although having powers to fight Garrick and the Imperials would be an added bonus.

"I'll ask her after dinner."

Markus's lips lifted in a sensual, yet dangerous smile. "Make that breakfast tomorrow. I have plans for you the rest of today, this evening, and tonight."

Desire tingled in her belly, then spread through her like a wildfire. Gods, she couldn't wait to get him all to herself.

Zavier cleared his throat. "Gwen also needs time to read the journal for more info."

Gwen took a breath and pushed away the desire, for now. "I'll keep searching. I want Garrick stopped as much you guys do."

Markus walked around the desk, stopped in front of her, and leaned against it. Zavier closed his laptop and quietly left the room. It made Gwen wonder if the two men used their brotherly-telepathic abilities with one another.

However, she didn't have time to ask. Markus took the tablet from her and set it on the desk behind him, out of her reach. "You are still low on energy."

"I feel fine."

Leaning forward, he placed his hands on the chair arms and caged her in. "No, you're not. As a love goddess, you need sex to recharge."

Her heart skipped a beat, then pounded like it was in her head. "I do not," she squeaked, making Markus grin.

Damn, sexy dragon.

"Shall I call Aphrodite and ask her?"

Gwen shook her head.

"Why not?"

Staring into his dragon-like gaze, she whispered. "Because I already know."

He inched closer and brushed his lips against her cheek and she fought a whimper and the need to rub up against him. Inhaling deeply, she closed her eyes. The draw to him grew stronger each day. She didn't understand it. She barely knew him, yet her body didn't care.

His kiss was quick and soft before he pulled back. Opening her eyes, she watched him extend his hand to her. "Come, take a walk with me."

She placed her hand in his and allowed him to pull her up with the trust she'd never felt for anyone in her life, except for her parents and Elle.

Markus led Gwen down the path toward the beach. He loved the ocean during the early evening. With the sun hidden by the mountain behind them, the whole section of beach was cast in a shadow, making the sand and the water seem darker.

Beside him, Gwen drew in a deep breath and sighed. "I love the ocean." When she looked up at him, she let out a soft, musical laugh. "I guess I told you that already."

His lips tugged into a smile as he ran his knuckles down her cheek and watched her lean into his touch. "What else do you love?"

She tilted her head. "I don't think there is anything that I don't love." Her brows dipped as she frowned and added, "Beside Garrick and anyone out to harm my family and friends."

Markus smiled again and couldn't remember the last time he'd smiled like this. There was a time that he was content with life enough to be happy, but never felt so alive just by being near someone.

"Go for a swim with me?"

Gwen looked around the beach, then to the ocean. "You're serious? I don't have a swimsuit."

He waggled his brows. "You don't need one."

Her eyes grew round and she stepped back. "You mean skinny dip? In the ocean?"

Irritation started to set in, dampening his good mood. "Are you chicken?"

She bit her bottom lip, which made his cock twitch behind the zipper of his jeans, and glanced at the water. "Is this beach private?"

He nodded. A shy smile formed on her lips as she stepped closer to him. "Do something for me first?"

Unfolding his arms, he wrapped them around her waist and drew her into him. "What does my little love goddess want?"

Her nose scrunched up at the title, and she flatted her hands on the chest. "Change into your dragon."

Drawing back, he studied her. There was no fear in the blue depths of her eyes, just curiosity. "Are you sure?"

Her head bobbed up and down. "I need to get over my fears. I trust you, even in the short time that we've known each other. If I agree to have sex with you to gain my strength back, I need to be able to accept all of you."

He pressed a kiss to her forehead, then stepped back, knowing her eyes never left him while he stripped. Her gaze caressed his naked skin and, gods, if it didn't feel like a physical touch.

Fuck. His body warmed and his skin tingled, needing her hands on him.

Once his clothes were removed, he turned and walked about twenty feet from her. He didn't want his tail or wings injuring her as he shifted. Turning to face her, he spread his arms. Usually he could shift in a matter of seconds, sometimes faster, depending on the situation, but right now he wanted to take it slow.

Mostly because he didn't want to scare her.

"What are you waiting on?" she called out, teasing.

The corner of his lips lifted as he visualized his dragon in his head. It was an automatic process. One he'd been born knowing, since he was never a child and most things came naturally to him and his brothers.

Giving into his dragon and allowing the beast to take

over, he completed the transformation. The burn of power grew from the center of his chest then shot out in all directions as his body grew and changed in a flash of black and blue.

Extending his wings, he stretched them wide before folding them back into his body. He stared down the beach and spotted Gwen where he'd left her. Only now she appeared to be closer due to the fact he was now the size of a passenger train car.

Lowering his large body into the warm sand, he waited—hoping she wouldn't have a panic attack—for her to approach him. It was ten painfully slow minutes before she approached. Excitement he never knew before filled him at her acceptance.

Hesitation slowed her steps and when stopped about a foot away from his snout, she just stared.

Growing impatient, Markus sent her a thought, unsure if it would work. Although he could connect telepathically with his brothers and the gods with ease, he wasn't so sure it would be the same with Gwen. Yet there was always a small chance it would, considering she was almost a full-blooded goddess herself.

I will not harm you. Besides it is killing me to hold onto my patience for much longer.

Surprise lit up her face, showing she heard his thoughts. "How?"

I can communicate to most gods and my brothers through thought.

Her blue eyes danced with delight and he wanted to

kiss her. "I'm not a goddess."

A growl rumbled through him and she stepped back. He sighed and laid his head on the sand. *Come here, Gwen.*

With her hand extended, she stepped forward until her palm touched his nose. Smiling, she ran her hand down the side of his jaw. "You are incredibly soft."

Thanks, I think.

Gwen laughed and relaxed her shoulders. "It is a compliment. I expected the scales to be rough, but they almost feel like soft leather."

With her hand still on him, she walked along his side. He turned his head so he could watch her. Stopping where his wings started, she ran a careful hand over the joint and down the edge of his wing. He shuddered, making her jerk her hand away.

Don't stop. That feels good.

"Oh." A glimpse of pink appeared in her cheeks.

Would you like to fly?

She twisted back around, her eyes lit with excitement. "Are you serious?"

He nodded his large head and extended a wing. *Just climb up. Don't worry, you can't hurt me. My wings are just as strong as my arms and legs.*

A nervous laugh escaped her as she slowly crawled onto his wing, then up his back. Settling herself between where his wings connected to his back, she rested her legs atop of his wings.

You ready?

"Yes," she said on a laugh that told him she was enjoying herself.

Good. He and his dragon loved it when she was smiling, calm, and happy, which they hadn't seen much since meeting her. They'd have to change that, he decided as he stood.

Gwen let out a squeak and laid on her belly and tried to hold onto his neck. Laughing in his head, he flapped his large wings and leaped in the air. It was always tricky taking off from the ground, but it was a skill he and each of his brothers had learned in order to be able to retreat at a moment's notice. Wind gusts coming off the mountain aided his lift off.

They flew over the ocean because it was safer than flying over the village. Even though the villagers knew about them and trusted them, they still feared their dragons. Markus and his brothers agreed not to expose their beasts too often in order to keep the residents of Serenity Cove peaceful and stress free. Especially with Garrick making the occasional appearance to plant fear in the people Markus and his brothers protected.

He hung a right a little sharper than he intended when a powerful gust of wind slammed into his left wing, lifting it up almost causing him to roll in the air. Gwen screamed and dug her nails into his neck. Markus gritted his teeth and pushed the sharp stabs of pain away. Leveling out, he headed back to the beach.

Markus slowed and landed on the sand, then settled so Gwen could slide off. When she came around to stand in front of him, her face looked a little pale. Shifting, he didn't bother with clothes. "Are you okay?"

With a wide smile on her face, she nodded. "That was amazing. A little frightening, but amazing."

He laughed and cupped her cheek. Satisfaction, along with something softer he couldn't name, filled him as she closed her eyes and leaned into his touch. Lowering his head, he pressed his forehead to hers. "Come swimming with me."

Opening her eyes, she nodded. "Okay."

Gwen started to remove her shirt as something flashed from the top of the cliff, drawing his attention. He placed a hand on her arm to stop her. Drawing her brows together, she glanced at him then turned to follow his gaze up. "Who is it?"

Markus growled, low. "Ashlynn."

"Do you want to go see what she's up to?"

He shook his head. "No. I'm sure Ty will follow her."

"What makes you say that?"

Meeting Gwen's blue gaze, he smiled "Because he's attracted to her."

Gwen smiled, then frowned. "He won't hurt her, will he?"

"No. Ty may not trust females, but he'd never harm one unless he's protecting himself or his family."

As if unsure, she turned back to peer up at the cliff's edge. Markus glanced up as well, in time to see Ashlynn disappear from sight.

Just to be safe, Markus sent a mental nudge to his brother. *Ty, Ashlynn is taking a walk.*

His brother replied instantly. *I'm on it.*

Satisfied that the female would be watched, Markus focused back on Gwen. "Still up for a swim?"

A slow smile lifted her sensual lips and she proceeded to remove her clothes. When she was done, she gave him a sexy grin before running toward the water. Delight bubbled up in his chest then turned into a need to chase her. He darted after her, running and jumping over the small waves as they broke on the shore.

When he caught up with her, he tackled her into the next, larger wave. When they surfaced, she laughed out loud and splashed water at him. "You'll pay for that, dragon."

He raised a brow. "Oh yeah? I look forward to it."

Closing the distance, he wrapped his arms around her and kissed her. A moan escaped her as she threaded her fingers through his hair, pulling slightly as she fisted a handful. He slid his hands down her back, over the curve of her ass and lifted her so she could wrap her legs around him, her pussy pinning his cock to his stomach. He thrust his tongue inside her mouth, making her move her hips against him, stroking his dick with each slow movement.

He trailed his hand further down her ass and between her thighs and slid one finger inside her. Her muscles tightened around him and she gasped against his lips then started sucking his tongue. Pleasure built to the point he almost came. Breaking the kiss, he kissed his way down her cheek to her neck while fingering her slick pussy.

Gwen tightened her grip in his hair and increased her rhythm against him. Pleasure built in a powerful wave until it crashed over them, pulling them under as an orgasm ripped through both of them.

Wrapping his arms around her to hold her still, he walked them to the shore and laid her down on the hard, wet sand. Bringing his hand to her face, he swiped a few strands of hair away and held her gaze. She was beautiful, her eyes half closed and her full lips slightly parted. Gods, he'd never have enough of her, he knew that now.

Now that he'd tasted her, he couldn't give her up.

Yet, in order to keep her it had to be true love. Hell, he didn't know what that was. Didn't know if the feeling growing inside him for this female was love or just affection or even an obsession.

Damn Aphrodite for implanting the little buzz in his ear about soul mates and true love not being a part of the curse.

Gwen frowned and cupped his cheek. "What's wrong?"

He lowered his head so his lips pressed into her palm. "Just thinking how beautiful you are and all the things I want to do to you." Lowering his head, he kissed her nose, then her lips. "And that I want to keep you for eternity."

CHAPTER SIXTEEN

Ash stepped into the forest around the dragons' mansion still amused at seeing Gwen and Markus on the beach. She'd stepped to the edge of the cliff just as Gwen climbed atop of Markus's dragon back and watched as he flew over the ocean with her. Enjoying the interaction and the huge smile on Gwen's face, Ash hovered too long at the edge. Her presence—even from the large distance between them—drew Markus's attention, surprising her.

The dragon most likely telepathically connected with one of his brothers—an ability she knew about, thanks to her mother—which was fine by her. Let one of the dragons follow her around. It didn't matter. She'd already told them she was a spy for the gods. What more did they want?

Continuing along the narrow path, she scanned the area for threats. The hairs on her arms stood to attention as a cool shiver rocked through her whole body. Someone was out here and it wasn't Markus or his brothers.

A moment later Garrick stepped onto the path in front of her, halting her in mid-step. *Fuck.* The murderous glare and pitch black eyes said he wasn't pleased.

"Evening, Ashlynn."

His voice glided over her skin like an oily residue and she held in a wince. "Garrick."

One side of his mouth lifted in an unamused, freak-ishly half-grin. Another shiver passed over her spine. When he took a step forward, Ash braced herself. If there was one thing she had learned from Garrick it was to never let her guard down.

Garrick was a sadistic prick on his good days.

"What have you been up to, my love?"

Breathe, Ash. Don't let your temper make things worse than they are. He only used endearments when he was trying to be charming and get something from her —whether it was information or sex, it didn't matter— or when there was someone else with them.

A breeze broke through the trees and with it came a scent that made her skin tingle—dark, sweet, and spicy. A scent she'd know anywhere, especially now that she knew to whom it belonged.

Not bothering to look around for Ty, she kept her gaze on Garrick. It really didn't matter, anyway. Garrick most likely knew his brother was near. It would explain why he hadn't attacked her, yet.

"Why are you here?" She took a slow and deliberate step back.

Like the predator he was, he tracked her movement, his dragon in his eyes. "I came for you. You don't really think that I'd let what is mine go so easily, do you?"

Fury reared its head, but Ash reined in her temper. *For now.* "I belong to no one."

Garrick, moving too fast for her to track, grabbed her upper arm and yanked her to him. The moment he did, a deep growl vibrated through the air around them and Garrick smiled. "I see someone has been a bad girl."

A spike of hot fear burned her belly and she was sure she would be sick. *Damn it, why couldn't Ty just go back to the mansion and mind his own business?*

She jerked, trying to break Garrick's hold on her. Laughing, he tightened his grip. His fingers dug into her muscles and she pressed her lips together to stop a cry from escaping. Pain pierced her arm and traveled down to her hand.

"Let me go," she demanded.

Garrick ignored her and scanned the forest around them. She did the same as much as she could with her side pressed against Garrick's. Ty was nowhere in sight, but she knew he was there, lurking. Somehow she could sense him, smell him, and feel him as if he was close enough to touch.

"I know you're there, brother." When Ty didn't show himself, Garrick added, "Ash, love, why don't you tell my brother who you belong to?"

Lifting her chin, she focused on a small empty space between two trees in front of her. It was where she sensed Ty the strongest. "I belong to no one. I'm a servant of the gods and only abide by their laws."

The slap came hard and fast. Garrick backhanded her, knocking her to the ground. Her chest tightened and lungs burned as she fought for air. The coppery taste of blood filled her mouth. Lifting her head, she glared up at Garrick through her hair. Just then, Ty flew from the shelter of the trees and tackled Garrick to the ground.

Ty got a good right hook on Garrick before the coward dematerialized. Ash watched as Ty stood, then roared. When he turned to her, she gasped then quickly averted her gaze. His sunglasses had fallen off when he attacked Garrick. The right side of his face around the eye was scarred, and his right eye was that of his dragon.

Ash took short, slow breaths in order to push through the pain. When she hit the ground, she'd landed on an exposed tree root.

Ty's booted feet came into view a moment before he squatted in front of her and offered his hand. When she lifted her head up, she stared into the dark lens of sunglasses. "What happened?"

"Garrick and his minions."

The words were clipped, saying that was all she was

getting from him. Yet, he still stood there with his hand out, palm up. Hesitantly, she placed hers in his and allowed him to pull her to her feet. The sudden movement made her dizzy and a little nauseous. When she swayed, Ty gripped her elbow with his other hand to steady her. Out of reflex, she placed a hand on his chest. Heat seeped into her palm and traveled up her arm. Desire bloomed within her.

Scowling, she stepped away from him and pulled her arm from his loose grasp. "Why are you following me?"

"Because we don't trust you."

She rolled her eyes and pushed past him. Ash had felt her mother's presence for a brief moment when Ty attacked Garrick and knew Artemis had abandoned the meeting for tonight.

Ty followed close behind her and growled. "What were you doing out here? Meeting Garrick and I spoiled things for you?"

Whirling around, she came nose to nose with the annoying dragon. "If you must know, I came to summon my mother."

A tic form in his temple. "Why?"

One. Two... "I'm a spy, remember? I have frequent meetings with Artemis." She turned and walked with quick strides back to the mansion.

~

GWEN STEPPED out of the shower, her body still tingling from making love to Markus on the beach. However, the bliss was pushed away by the annoying little voice known as a conscience, and the realization that she had feelings for him.

Grabbing the towel from the rack to her right, she tried to push thoughts of Markus out of her mind. She couldn't fall in love with him. He was an immortal shape-shifting god, and, as far as she knew, she was mortal. At least her dad was, or he'd be alive now.

Wouldn't he?

After drying off, she grabbed Markus's robe from the hook on the back of the bathroom door. His sensual, earthy scent reached out to her, tempting and alluring. Lifting the terry cloth to her nose, she inhaled. Flashes of their tangled bodies formed in her mind, and her skin heated all over again.

Damn, she was done for. She'd never be able to look at him again without wanting him. Which was ridiculous.

She wasn't a hormonal teen. She was an adult who happened to have the best sex of her life. That was all. It was just sex with the purpose of recharging her energy. And it worked.

Gwen had never felt better, more alive and recharged.

However, she couldn't have sex with Markus again. It was too much of a risk to her heart and her sanity.

Replacing the robe on the hook, she exited the bathroom and entered the walk-in closet where she dressed in a pair of jeans and a pink turtleneck sweater. She didn't bother with her hair, deciding to let it dry naturally. Besides she didn't have plans to do anything the rest of the evening but read through her father's journals.

She damn sure wasn't going to seek out Markus.

With a sigh, she picked up the tablet from the dresser and settled into the oversized armchair next to the French doors that opened onto a terrace. She considered grabbing a blanket and sitting outside, but clouds had darkened the sky by the time she and Markus returned to the house, indicating there was a storm heading their way.

On that thought, she got up and opened the twin glass doors and smiled as the sounds of the ocean waves and the smell of the cool, salty air drifted into the room.

Sitting back down in the chair, she powered on the tablet and opened the file to her father's journal entries.

October 15, 1977

Today Garrick surprised me by telling me he could unlock my godly powers. I laughed at first, thinking he was joking, but he wasn't. Intrigued, I asked him to explain.

He told me he discovered a serum that, when injected into the bloodstream, could unlock powers. He said he'd done it on himself and a few others and ensured it was safe. When I hesitated, he called another man into the room and proceeded to inject him with the serum.

When the other man didn't drop dead and confirmed his powers were indeed unlocked, I wanted to try it. I mean, I am a demi-god and deserve to enjoy the benefits of the godly magic I was born with. Besides, if my theory is correct, I'll be able to find others like me once in full control of my powers.

The rush of energy like I've never felt before was incredible. My mind is fully open to every sound, every sight, and a vision of the future flashed in my mind's eye. Alexia and I will be blessed with a daughter soon.

I can't wait to meet her and share my discoveries with her.

A knock on the door brought Gwen's head up. Frowning, she rose and went to the door and then smiled wide. "Elle."

She drew her sister into a hug. Pulling back, Gwen studied the other woman. Her pale green eyes sparkled with satisfaction and it made Gwen curious to what her sister and BFF had been up to. "What is it?"

Elle motioned toward the room. Gwen stepped aside to allow her to come in and shut the door behind them. "Now, spill. You are too wired for some reason."

"It's not what you think." Elle laughed. "I've been painting. I had the most bizarre dream two nights ago. It's inspired a whirlwind of paintings and drawings."

"That's great. But why are we speaking softly behind a closed door?"

Dropping her shoulders, Elle stepped closer and whispered. "I'm not sure what they mean. It's hard to explain. I've never had this type of drive to paint before. When I finished the first five, I saw it. A pattern and similarities in each one."

A sinking, almost sick feeling churned in Gwen's belly. Elle's excitement suddenly turned to alarm, which set off Gwen's warning bells. She took her sister's hand and tugged her to the bed and sat. "Just tell me, Elle. I'm past the panic attacks. I think being here with the dragons and seeing how they are not evil helped."

Elle nodded. "Yes, I can see that. The Sons of War have good souls. Well, as good as they can as dragons." She gave a nervous laugh before continuing. "The painting are all dark and, at a glance, look like something that should belong to a fantasy art show. But when I looked closer, I can see the truth in them."

Gwen shook her head, trying to understand. "You're not making much sense. Please, Elle, explain."

Elle sighed. "It may be better if you saw them for yourself."

"Okay, let's go." Gwen stood and waited for Elle, who was a little slower and seemed a little reluctant to go down to her studio in the basement.

Folding her arms, Gwen meet Elle's gaze. "You're scaring me. First you were excited, now you're hesitant. What is going on?"

Elle looked down at her hands. "The paintings seem

to tell a story. It's like each one is a different event, but I can't tell if they are past events or future ones."

"How many did you paint?"

Elle met her gaze. "About a dozen or so, a few unfinished, and some sketches."

"Okay, do you think it'd be helpful if Markus saw them too?"

Elle shrugged. "Maybe."

Gwen sighed. "Come on, then, let's go find the head dragon and go look at your paintings."

Inwardly, Gwen groaned because she was really hoping that she could avoid Markus for at least a day or two before she was forced to face him.

CHAPTER SEVENTEEN

M arkus stared in disbelief at the row of paintings. Each scene told the story of the Sons of War as the events happened over a thousand years ago.

The first one was of Ares with his son, the *Drakon Ismenios*, dead at his feet. The dragon's teeth scattered over the ground. The next scene depicted the warriors rising from the earth in rows that extended as far back as he could see.

Gwen shifted from foot to foot beside him. "Are those the Sons of War?"

Markus nodded. "Yes. The *Drakon's* teeth were divided into two groups. My brothers and I were of the first group. This group."

He felt Gwen's gaze before she asked, "How do you know?"

"Because Ares hid the second set in Tartarus."

"Where are all the Sons?"

Markus sighed. "Most died. A few left Olympus. Only the six of us stayed."

They fell silent as they studied the rest of the paintings. The next several were different scenes from the war against the gods and their earth-bound children. The paintings were life-like and so detailed. It was like Markus was sucked back in time.

Each painting featured either him or his brothers.

He came to a stop at the last one, Garrick in dragon form. His large black wings extended as if preparing to take flight. Moving closer to the painting, Markus focused on the small sack-like item in the dragon's claw.

"Elle, in your dreams, did you hear anything?"

"Sometimes," Elle shrugged. "It wasn't always clear."

Markus pointed at the canvas. "Do you know what is in that sack?"

Elle's eyes grew wide and she nodded. "The *drakon's* teeth."

Fuck.

"Ares!" Markus shouted. A few moments later, the god materialized in cloud of dark gray smoke.

At first, he appeared annoyed at being summoned, but when he saw the paintings, he froze. "What in the name of Zeus?"

Markus drew his brows together. "Elle's been having dreams."

Ares turned to Elle. When Gwen stepped in front of her friend, Ares laughed. "I do not wish to harm her. I'm just curious."

Markus moved closer to the females. "Please tell me that the last painting is not the present."

Ares narrowed his eyes, then let out a low growl. "No. The other set of teeth are in Tartarus with Typhon."

Typhon, a storm daemon, was the gatekeeper and warden of the fire pit of the Underworld. Markus wasn't so sure he liked the idea of a daemon guarding the *drakon's* teeth. "You trust him?"

Ares raised a brow. "Do I trust anyone?

"But a daemon?"

"He's bound to Tartarus and can't leave without suffering a very painful death. Besides, anyone seeking the teeth would have to get past Hades first." Ares turned back to the paintings. "However, nothing is a hundred percent and there are ways around the most difficult challenges. You must keep an eye on your brother. Ashlynn will know how."

Before Markus could ask any more questions, Ares dematerialized.

He scrubbed a hand over his face. "Fuck, I hate when he does that. Why can't he just answer my damn questions?"

When he looked up, the females stared at him. Elle

had her bottom lip sucked in and Gwen had hers pressed together. Both of them had laughter in their eyes. "It's not funny."

Gwen shook her head. "No, it's not." She turned to Elle. "Where is the unfinished one?"

With worry in her gaze, Elle made her way to the corner of the room that was now her studio and uncovered a canvas. Once the painting was in his full view, Markus let out another curse and bent forward to get a closer look.

In the center was a sketch of a woman in a long flowing gown. The dress was pulled tight around the female's figure and flowed behind as if she stood in high winds. Her hair blew in the same direction with a few thick strands in her face.

The background was the only color, but he could tell why since it still wasn't finished. It lacked the depth and details of the other paintings.

"Elle, please explain this one."

Stepping up beside him, she cleared her throat. "I'm not sure, but I think she's a storm daemon. In my dream, she called a storm. That's what all the clouds are behind her. There will be lightening all around her, and below her will be the sea, angry and ready to obey her."

Markus studied the female on the canvas. She looked familiar, but he couldn't be sure with only a rough sketch. "Let me know when you finish it."

Elle nodded, then covered the painting again. "I will." She hesitated a moment, then said, "I've never had visions. Sure, I see night creatures, but that is expected since my great-gr...my mother is Nyx. These dreams could be my imagination running wild because the myths I learned are coming to life."

Gwen took Elle's hand as if comforting her friend. "I agree. We've been under a lot of stress these last couple of days."

Although they had a logical point, Markus thought something else was going on. "Just continue to paint and draw anything you dream about. I'm curious to see where this goes. If you don't have these dreams again, then I'll dismiss it as an overactive imagination."

Turning, he walked to the door, then stopped and looked back at Gwen. "Meet me in the training room in fifteen minutes."

Leaving the studio, Markus smiled. Gwen thought she could avoid him, but she was wrong. Besides she made a deal to train with him and have dinner with him. He was going to see she kept her word and take every opportunity to seduce her into being his mate.

Because that was exactly what she was, his one true soul mate. The knowledge slammed into him hard right after his mind cleared from the multiple orgasms they shared on the beach.

Now that he'd had a taste of her, he wanted to bond with her.

And nothing, or no one, was going to get in his way of having what he wanted.

GWEN CROUCHED LOW, waiting, watching.

When Markus's muscles flexed and he lifted a foot, she was ready, mimicking his movements. Yet, she was still too slow. In one swift movement, he tackled her on the mat. Her back hit hard and she gasped more out of reflex then actual pain, but it made Markus pause long enough for her to roll from under him.

Pushing to a stand, she darted toward him and wrapped an arm around his neck in a choke hold.

He grunted and held his hands up. "You think you're smart?"

Gwen released him and straightened. "No. Just took advantage of the weak point."

Slowly, he stood and turned to face her. "Your real opponent won't care if he slams you a little too hard on the floor."

"That's the point of this, isn't it? To build up my strength?"

He stared at her for several moments, studying her as if tossing around a theory in his head or something. "You'd be stronger if your powers were unbound."

Shocked, she held his gaze. "What?"

One side of his mouth lifted. "Look, you are stronger then you were before coming here. Emotionally, you've overcome your fear of dragons. You're almost able to outwit me, but you'll never be strong enough as a mortal."

She propped her hands on her hips. "And how do you plan on doing that? Isn't it against the rules or something? I mean, there was a reason why the descendants' powers were locked."

"Mainly to keep them from rising against the gods again."

Relaxing her arms to her sides, she watched him, not sure what to expect. Maybe he was joking. The idea of having her powers unlocked was a little scary. What if she couldn't handle it?

"Do you know how?"

"No, but Ashlynn might."

She opened her mouth to ask why he thought so, then remembered the passage she'd read in her father's journal entries earlier that day. "Because Garrick is unlocking their powers."

He raised a brow. "How do you know?"

She told him about the journal entry. "When Elle came up to the room and told me about the painting, it slipped my mind."

His dark blue eyes flashed to the light blue of his dragon as he took a step toward her. Her heart hammered hard in her chest and she felt it in her throat. Stepping back, she tripped on the edge of the mat and fell on her ass. Markus dropped to his knee and caged her.

Fear burned through her, bringing back a panic attack. Her chest tightened and she fought to catch her breath. The next moment she was pulled into Markus's arms, her head against his chest. She focused on the *thump, thump* of his heart to calm her.

Embarrassed and pissed off at herself for not having a better handle over her anxiety, she closed her eyes tight to keep the tears from falling. Markus pressed a kiss to the top of her head, then her temple.

"I'm sorry. I didn't think." Drawing her closer, he tightened his arms a little and rubbed soothing circles on her back.

Taking a shaky breath, she whispered, "I'm never going to be normal."

"Love, you're a goddess. You were never normal."

That made her laugh, because he had a point.

They fell silent for several long moments before she pulled away. She frowned at the wet spot on his shirt and reached out and smoothed the cotton with her hand. Before she could turn away, Markus cupped her cheek and raised her chin so she met his gaze.

"You must never fear me."

"I don't."

"Then what just happened?"

"I...you caught me off guard. I felt your annoyance and I must have mistaken it for anger."

Still holding her face in his hands, he pressed his forehead to hers. "I was annoyed you withheld the information from me, but I'm not angry. Despite the fact that there's a fire breathing dragon inside me, it takes a lot more than that to make me mad at you." He lifted his head and stared into her eyes. "I could never harm you, even if my own life depended on it."

Something different reached out to her senses. It wasn't fear or anger. Acceptance? No, it was stronger. Almost like affection. "What do you mean?"

"You are my one true mate."

CHAPTER EIGHTEEN

G wen opened her mouth, then closed it, unable to form the words swirling around in her mind.

His mate? It wasn't the first time he'd told her, but the way he said the single word held a lot more meaning than just a wife or a partner. Gods, she couldn't mate with him. Not with his evil brother hunting her down, and not even if Garrick wasn't.

Yet, it was exactly what she wanted deep down.

Shaking all over, she turned and ran from the room.

When she reached the third floor of the mansion, she dropped down into the reading chair next to the large bay windows and watched the ocean in the distance. So much had happened in such a short time that she needed to think, away from Markus. His scent, hell, his whole presence, confused her.

A shift of power in the air warned that Aphrodite had materialized behind her. Gwen recognized the goddess's magical signature. It was warm, loving, and so much like her father's that it brought tears to her eyes. She took a deep breath and waited for her grandmother to sit next to her.

Aphrodite took her hand and linked their fingers together. "The ocean is beautiful."

Gwen just nodded, not trusting her voice at the moment. So they sat for the longest time, not speaking. After a while Aphrodite opened the windows by using her mind, which drew Gwen's attention to her.

Turning to face her grandmother, Gwen offered a weak smile. She had Aphrodite's blue eyes and blond hair. Gwen could see where her father got his looks from. "I can't mate with Markus."

Aphrodite smiled and cupped her cheek. "Sure you can, but it is your choice."

Gwen searched her blue gaze in confusion. "I guess I don't understand what he meant by his 'one true mate.'"

The goddess shook her head. "I think you do, but you're too scared to admit it."

Looking away, Gwen shrugged. "I know what the phrase means by definition. I don't know what it involves. The rules? Is the myth true—the Sons of War couldn't mate with the descendants?"

Aphrodite sighed and stared out the open windows. "The mythology is true. Yet, like all laws, the wording is what is important."

Gwen glanced over at her profile and thought about

it. The Sons weren't allowed to mate with the descendants. Markus said she was his one true mate. Didn't it mean the same thing?

Damn, she was too tired and sore from the training session with Markus to think.

After a few moments, Aphrodite let out a breath. "As much as he would like to, Zeus can't control free will. If the Fates deemed you two are mates…"

Of course! "Then the curse is canceled out."

Aphrodite smiled, wide. "Now you're catching on. All you have to do is search in your heart and accept the mating."

Accept the mating?

Before Gwen could ask another question, her grandmother was gone, dematerialized to wherever she went after leaving her side.

Gwen sighed, stood and walked to the windows. The roar of the ocean filled the air like nature's song. All she had to do was accept the mating, huh?

How could she commit to someone who didn't love her?

MARKUS ENTERED his study and growled at the sight of his brothers. Seth and Ty were lounging on the sofa. Well, Ty lounged. Seth was playing a video game with the sound up loud enough to give Markus a headache.

Zavier and Drake sat at the small round table to the

right of Markus's desk. Each of them had their laptops opened and it appeared they were collaborating about something.

"Out of all the rooms in this house, you have to be in *my* study?" Markus grumbled as he made his way to his desk and sat down.

Ty spoke, but didn't look in Markus's direction. "I called a meeting and figured it'd be more private in here considering we have a guest."

Markus settled back into his chair and studied his brother. There was something bothering Ty. Markus guessed it had something to do with Ashlynn. If so, then Ty wouldn't be sharing with the group anytime soon.

"What is this about?"

Ty glanced over at Markus. "I followed the female like you asked. She said she was meeting her mother, but Garrick showed up instead."

"Do you think she lied?"

Ty shook his head. "No. She spoke the truth." One side of his mouth lifted. "I got a good hit on the bastard before he flashed out of there."

Seth turned off the game and faced everyone. "Gary's a chicken-shit. We need to get a big net for the next time he shows up."

Markus's stomach soured at Seth's words. "What makes you think he'll be back?"

Seth shrugged and stood, then stretched. "It's just a hunch, but he may have come in search of Ash. Why else would he show up in the forest while she was out there?"

Ty nodded. "He did come for her and might have taken her if I wasn't there." His eyes glowed behind his shades and he set his jaw, making the muscle in his temples flex. "Gary knew I was there and claimed Ash belongs to him."

Markus narrowed his gaze on Ty. It was the first time the male called the huntress by her nickname. "He could have been taunting you."

Ty's gaze snapped to Markus's. "I don't give a shit either way, but I'll be damned if the son of a bitch will come to my home and think he can just take whomever he pleases. He won't get any of the females inside these walls."

Markus stared at Ty, wondering what wound his brother up so tight. Usually he didn't care much about females. His behavior seemed almost protective. It was a little out of character for Ty, especially since he returned to them from his captivity with the Imperials.

Before Markus could call him on the personality shift, the door to the study opened and Gwen rushed in, tablet in hand, and skidded to halt in the middle of the room and scanned her surroundings. "Oh. I'm sorry." She turned to leave, but Markus teleported to stand in the open door.

"What is it?"

Gwen took a step back. "I didn't mean to interrupt. I…"

Markus cut her off by closing in the gap between them, wrapping an arm around her, and kissing her. Instantly, she melted into him and fisted a hand into his hair. The gentle tugs on his hair sent sparks of desire through him and straight to his dick, which had went impossibly hard the moment she walked into the room.

One of his brothers cleared his throat, reminding Markus they had an audience. Breaking the kiss, he held Gwen's desire filled gaze.

"What did you find?" He pointed to the tablet, obviously the reason behind her rushed entrance.

Embarrassment colored her cheeks as she looked around the room and ducked her head. With shaky hands, she sat on one of the chairs in front of his desk. "The passage I'm about to read is why Garrick killed my father."

Gwen ignored the muttered curses and started reading from her father's journal.

November 10, 1978

It's been hard to stay away from home ever since Gwendolyn arrived in June. She's perfect and has her grandmother's nose and bright blue eyes, but her mother's chin and fingers. Alexia and I are so blessed to have such a healthy and happy baby girl.

Each day, I spend a little longer leaving the house to go to work. Garrick grumbled about it a few times, but never threatened me with the loss of a job because of it.

Today was especially hard. Last night I had the most disturbing dream about a war. This war was not on

Earth, not that I could tell anyway. The land seemed ancient and otherworldly. My gut told me it was Olympus. Aphrodite was there. As were Ares, Zeus, and even Hades. The gods had an army of warriors who could shift into dragons. They fought against humans with godly powers, much like the ones I and the other Imperials have.

That's what Garrick calls us. The Imperials— blessed mortals who pledge to watch over the rest of the humans. I've always thought Garrick had a strange way about him, but he was smart and shared my views on finding the descendants.

At least I believed that up until a few days ago when I unlocked a file on Garrick's computer. I found lists of names, birthdays, locations, and the name of a god next to each name. I recognized most of the names as members of the Imperials, since I work beside them every day.

Then the dream last night caused more suspicion because the last face I saw before waking was Garrick's.

I rushed to the office and was relieved when no one else was there. I quickly brought up the file from the other day and searched through others. The more I dug, the sicker I felt. Garrick wasn't searching for the descendants to keep them safe and inform them of their heritages, he was gathering an army to wage a war against the gods.

Gwen stopped reading and pressed the screen with her finger then turned the tablet around for them to see.

Markus's heart dropped to the floor. Dread burned through him as he stared at the photo of the female storm daemon dressed in a flowing black gown with dark storm clouds rolling in the background.

It was so close to the unfinished painting Elle showed him that morning that Markus was betting it was the same. Only in this colored photo, Markus could see clearly enough to recognize the daemon.

Sophia, the daughter of Typhon—storm daemon and guardian of Tartarus—and the female Garrick killed over a thousand years ago. It was why they were banished from the Heavens and cursed.

Markus meet Gwen's gaze. "Has Elle seen this?"

She shook her head. "This is a digital drawing from a seer within the Imperials. Father's notes go on to say that Sophia was Garrick's mate and the seer confirmed she was still alive and living as a human on earth."

Seth stepped closer, shaking his head. "This is impossible. We saw her decapitated body. Typhon almost broke out of Tartarus to wipe us all out because of it."

Gwen handed the tablet to Zavier as he came to study the device. "There's a hidden file I opened when I accessed this journal entry. It has a lot of information about Sophia and Garrick, their relationship, her death, and a prophecy of her rebirth as a human."

Zavier took the tablet and scanned through the information. "Can I take this and read through the entries?"

Gwen nodded. "What does it mean if he finds her? Would she know who she was if she was reborn?"

Markus raked a hand through his hair. "Typically, in theory no. When a god is killed and reborn as a mortal, they have no memory of their past life." *Fuck.* He turned toward the door and walked out into the foyer and called out, "Ashlynn!"

A moment later the redhead descended the stairs. "Why must you yell? My hearing is as good as yours."

When he narrowed his eyes at her, she raised a brow and confirmed his suspicions that she was a full goddess. Knowing Ty, the male had already called her out on the lie. That could be the only reason she let her shields down now. "What do you know of Sophia?"

Ash drew her brows together. "Sophia who?"

"Storm daemon."

"She's dead."

"Not according to two seers." Elle wasn't a gifted seer, but Ash didn't need to know Elle was the second to visualize the daemon alive.

Ashlynn descended the last step and motioned toward the study. "I hate repeating myself, so we might as well make a party of it."

CHAPTER NINETEEN

Ash walked through the door and leaned against the wall, arms folded. The glares she kept sending Ty told Gwen she wasn't happy to be there. At least not happy to be in the same room as Ty.

"I heard that Sophia had been reborn as a mortal. Most believe she has no memories of her life as a storm daemon. I've heard Artemis say that it was all a part of the 'banish the dragons and please her father by bringing her back to life' curse." Ash glanced to Markus and rolled her eyes.

Markus crossed his arms over his chest. "Is that it?"

Ash let out a breath. "I was a little girl at the time. They didn't exactly speak about that kind of stuff directly to me."

Seth whistled. "Man, that would make you…"

"Old," Ash said sternly, cutting him off. "But not as old as you guys."

Seth laughed. "Aged to perfection, baby."

Ash rolled her eyes again.

Markus said, "She's Garrick's mate, or at least she used to be."

Sagging against the wall, Ash shook her head. "He only talked about her when he was mad at me and thought he was making me jealous. I don't think he knows where she is. Besides, Zeus would make sure she was well hidden."

"Meaning she doesn't know who she is," Markus said.

"And she may not have her powers," Ty added.

Drake spoke for the first time since Gwen came to the study. "Sophia is a pretty common name and, knowing the God King, he'd give her a last name just as common."

Markus paced the floor. "So she's not a threat, not yet. Zavier, go ahead and search for her, but don't make it a priority. We have to find the two women on that list and keep Gwen and Elle off Garrick's radar."

"I could go back in," Ash said.

Ty snorted. "Yeah, like he'd believe you. You told him you were a spy."

Ash smiled, but it held no humor. "I told him I was a servant of the gods, but he doesn't believe that shit."

Markus shook his head. "No, we'll find another way."

Gwen stood, drawing everyone's attention. "Then she'll take me as her prisoner."

"Absolutely not."

Markus's sharp tone made Gwen shrink back a little. Then it pissed her off. Where did he get off, telling her no? "You didn't even hear me out. Do you always say no before hearing the whole plan?"

Unfolding his arms, he closed the distance between them. "I don't care what the plan is. I don't want you anywhere near him."

Gwen placed her hands on her hips and stood on her toes to try to be at his level. "If my powers were unlocked, I could fight him."

The muscles in his cheeks tightened, making his features more defined. "The answer is no."

Ty cleared his throat. "She may be our chance to grab some valuable information and files."

Markus whirled around and let out a growl. Out of instinct, Gwen gripped his arm. When he turned back to her, his dragon peeked through. A hint of fear spiked, but she didn't release him or back down. "I can help. With both Ash and me in there, we could even booby-trap the place and set him back a little."

"You know she has a point." Ash pushed off the wall. "I can call Garrick and grovel a little, feed him bullshit, and tell him I could deliver Gwen to him. I know he'll fall for it. He's so hard up to get his hands on her, he'll be even more so when I tell him she belongs to you."

Gwen gaped at Ash. Did everyone know she and Markus were mates?

Markus stalked toward Ash. Ty was right beside him in a flash with his hand on his brother's arm. Markus rolled his shoulder, breaking Ty's hold. "Only one problem."

"What's that?"

Markus growled out, "I don't know how to unlock her powers."

"I do." Ash smiled like a cat that locked the dog out of the house.

"Care to share?" Markus raised a brow

"With your blood."

Markus jerked back. "That'll bind her to me for the rest of her life."

"Then you two have much to discuss." Ash shrugged. "If you don't mind, I'm going back to my room. While I'm there, I'll try to summon Artemis. She may be able to give me some advice or just tell me I'm crazy. Hell, maybe she'll feel sorry for me and take me home."

On the heels of her words, she turned and left the study.

Markus turned to Gwen and she was glad to see that his eyes were human again. "Everyone out."

His brothers left without another word. Seth shut the door with a wink and a big grin. Gwen, on the other hand, shook all over. She didn't want to make this choice now. But she would if it meant it brought them one step closer to bringing Garrick down for his crimes.

MARKUS WATCHED Gwen fidget with a loose string on the hem of her thigh length sweater. Her confusion and desire reached out to him like a sensually sweet cocktail. When he stepped closer, her fingers stilled.

With a sigh, he dropped to his knees in front of her and covered her hand with his. "I'll answer all your questions."

She lifted her lashes to meet his gaze. "I'm not sure where to begin. So much has happened in a very short amount of time."

A tiny spark of hope lit up within him and he clung onto it. "I'm immortal and very old. Time means very little to me, but I'm also unsure about the future. I'd never considered taking a mate."

Her shoulders dropped a little as she seemed to relax, but she still held him at a distance he and his dragon didn't care for. "Me either. I mean who would want to commit to a woman afraid of her own shadow? Most people think I'm crazy."

A playful growl rumbled from him. "You are not crazy. You're beautiful, smart, and sexy."

Her cheeks turned pink and she averted her gaze. "The only thing I'm sure about is that I want Garrick to pay for taking my parents from me."

Her blue eyes had darkened and he could see determination in the depths. "Unlocking your powers with my blood will link us together."

She tilted her head. "But it's different than a mating bond?"

"Yes. It won't be as strong, but you can still be sensitive to me. You may even be able to send me telepathic messages, not just hear mine."

"That doesn't sound too bad. I mean, I'm not sure I'm ready to be your mate. It's just…I can't commit to a loveless relationship."

Markus's heart stuttered behind his ribs and his dragon snarled at her admission. "It won't be loveless."

"What are you saying?"

"I'm not sure if I know what love is or if I'm capable of it. I know I want to keep you safe. You're all I think about and I can't imagine ever letting you go. Is that love?"

She stared at him far too long for his patience. When he reached the point where he wanted to grab her by the shoulders and make her speak, she let out a soft sigh. "I think so."

"Do you feel the same way?"

"Yes, but I don't know anything about you. Your likes, dislikes."

Her words cut off when he cupped her face and pressed his lips to hers in a soft, quick kiss. "We have eternity to learn them about each other. You are my mate and I'm sure the Fates aren't wrong about these things."

Drawing back slightly, she studied him for several moments before she smiled and pressed her forehead to his. "How long will I need to train before going with Ash?"

"I never agreed to that plan."

A soft laugh drifted from her lips. "You were thinking about it. Look, I know the dangers. Hell, the whole idea scared the shit out of me, but I can't just not do it. I have the chance to strike back and I *need* to."

He pushed away the dread and the primal need to lock her up until Garrick was dealt with. "With Aphrodite's help, I can have you ready in three days."

"Then let's get started with unlocking my powers."

"It's not going to be easy. I'll push you to your breaking point to prepare you. Garrick is a mean-ass bastard."

"Whatever it takes."

With a sigh, he stood and lifted her up in his arms. "I'll agree to this on one condition."

"What's that?"

"That you become my bonded mate on the third night, then on the fourth we go in."

She thought about it for a brief moment, then nodded. "Deal."

CHAPTER TWENTY

Gwen's heart thumped so hard in her chest she thought the thing would leap out. Everything was happening so fast, yet it all felt so right. If she was truly going insane, she'd go out of her mind with a bang.

Their gazes locked as Markus laid her down on his bed. "So how does this work?"

His sensual mouth twitched. "I have no clue."

Lowering his head, he captured her lower lip between his teeth and gave a gentle tug. A groan escaped as tingles of desire danced over her skin. Gods, she never knew a simple bite on the lip could make her beg for more, but one from Markus did.

She wrapped her legs around his hips and pulled him closer, needing to feel him close. When he broke the kiss and drew back, she held the dragon-like gaze and smiled. For the first time since meeting him, she didn't have the urge to run or pull away. Now she knew the dragon, had ridden on his back over the ocean, and touched his scales and wings.

That dragon belonged to her. Somehow she knew it in the depths of her soul. The dragon was her protector, and the man was her lover and friend. The sudden realization of what Aphrodite had tried to tell her earlier that day slammed into her. Her heart bloomed with acceptance and something much deeper.

Love.

"Gwen?"

Stunned, she focused on Markus and frowned. His brows were drawn together and his forehead crinkled as if concerned about something. Cupping his face in her hands, she tugged his head down and kissed him. Pulling away, she stared into his midnight blue gaze. "I'm fine. Promise. Everything's going to okay."

One dark brow rose and he asked, "Did you have a vision?"

It was logical for him to think she did, since her father had visions. "No. It was more of a knowing. I'm falling in love with you."

His eyes went round and the color brightened slightly. "Really? Then you feel the connection, the urge to mate?"

She wasn't sure if she'd describe it like that, but it was pretty close. "I think so."

A sensual smile formed and damn if it didn't make her skin heat up and pussy pulse with need. "Careful what you say. To complete the mating bond, all you have to do is fully accept me as your mate while tasting my blood."

She returned his smile. "Then let's do it."

"Are you sure?"

Nodding, she raised her head and nipped at his bottom lip. "I'm sure."

He growled and slipped his hand under her shirt and cupped her breast through her bra. In slow circular motions, she moved her hips against him, drawing a groan from both of them.

Gently, Markus reached back, grabbed her ankle, and she loosened her hold on him. He rose up on his knees, unfastened her jeans, and then slid them along with her panties down her legs. After removing her pants, he took her hand and pulled her to sit up. With one swift movement, he pulled her shirt over her head.

Laying back against the mattress in nothing but her black lace bra, she watched the man who heated her from the inside out. Holding her gaze, Markus lowered his head to her core and she held her breath. He stopped inches from her clit and she whimpered.

She would not beg, damn it.

A wicked smiled formed on his lips right before he closed the distance and covered her with his mouth. His tongue circled her clit and she cried out. Fisting the sheets she rode the hot, wild wave of the orgasm as it crashed over her.

Markus kissed his way up her body, stopping to remove her bra, and dipped his head to tease a nipple with his tongue. Pinpricks raced along each nerve ending, almost making her come again.

With feather-like touches, he slid his fingers down her side to her stomach. A shiver of anticipation went through her and her sex grew wetter the closer his fingers got. Finally, he dipped a finger inside her, making her gasp as a wave of pleasure crashed over her, pulling her under.

Markus rose above Gwen and gazed into her sky blue eyes. Desire he'd never known slammed into him, consuming and primal. He'd never known love before, but he was sure that was what he felt for this female. His chest ached and his dragon paced anxiously when she wasn't near. When she said she was falling in love with him, he almost ripped her clothes and claimed her right then.

No, he'd have to take it slow. Gwen was worth more than a hard fuck. At least for the mating ritual. Besides, he had a lifetime to take her hard and fast, and any other way he could.

"You're mine, always."

LIA DAVIS

She gave a nod, her eyes turning a deeper shade of blue. "Always."

Dipping his head, he captured her lips and thrust his tongue inside her mouth. Opening for him, she met his tongue with her own. Her fingers threaded through his hair and pulled, making him groan. His cock pressed painfully into the zipper of his jeans.

Breaking the kiss, he stood and removed his clothes. Meeting Gwen's hunger-filled gaze, he felt something inside open up. It was like a new understanding, or knowing filled his mind and senses. He could understand how a dragon could go insane if he lost his mate, because Markus felt a primal need to protect her.

Dread entered his thoughts, because he didn't want her to go forward with the crazy plan just to gain information about Garrick.

Gwen frowned as if she knew where his thoughts had gone and reached out for him and he went to her, lying down on his side next to her. "I can't lose you."

She cupped his face. "You won't."

"Why are we doing this again?"

"Set up a trap for Gary."

A laugh burst from his lips as she lifted her brows and crinkled her nose as she spoke the words. Plus the sound of Garrick's nickname on her lips made him laugh. "What if that doesn't work? Then I'll take whatever I can so we can better track him and try again later. We can't allow him to think we are weak. He needs to be stopped."

His lips twitched, pride blooming within his chest. She spoke like a warrior and with such drive and passion for her mission. It washed away some of his worry. This could work if they worked as a team, had a plan, and if he taught Gwen all she needed to know to come back to him alive.

Markus pressed his lips to hers and said against her mouth, "You are incredible."

Before she could reply, he bit her bottom lip, making her moan. When he rose and released a claw on his right hand to cut a small gash in his neck, Gwen gasped and grabbed his wrist. "What are you doing?"

""I'm going to cut my throat so you can take my blood as I take your body."

Her skin flushed and eyes darkened. She released him, but didn't speak as he broke the skin just enough that a small bead of blood formed.

Her gaze flicked to the cut, then to his eyes. As if the thought of tasting blood wasn't very appealing, she crinkled her nose. For him, it was a part of being a dragon. His beast craved it from time to time and he had to hunt down animals from the surrounding mountain areas.

"Just focus on me and not the taste."

She took a breath and nodded. "I trust you."

"I want you as my mate from this day forward. Do you accept me as your eternal mate?"

Her blue eyes sparked, first with confusion, then

with desire and acceptance. "Yes. I accept you and your dragon as mine for as long as I live."

Lifting her head, she pressed a kiss to his lips, then his jaw and continued until her mouth closed over the cut. Her gentle pulls on his skin sent a jolt of desire straight to his cock.

Sucking in a breath, he gripped his dick and guided himself to Gwen's entrance. She let out a little moan of encouragement and scored his back with her nails. *Fuck.* The stabs of pain turned to pleasure as she gently bit down on his throat. Abandoning the thought of taking it slow, he thrust deep inside her.

Gwen released his neck on a scream of pleasure, her nails gripping his back. When he picked up his rhythm, she screamed again as another orgasm rocked through her. His own tore through him, hard.

Withdrawing from her, he fell to his side next to her and squeezed her closer to him and kissed her forehead. "Do you feel different?"

A soft laugh escaped her and she wrapped her arms around him. "I feel wonderful, like jelly, but wonderful."

Laughing he poked her gently in the ribs, making her squeak and jerk away. "I meant your powers."

She shook her head and he could sense her worry through the mating bond. "No. It didn't work."

"Maybe it takes time."

"Maybe you just wore me out too much to notice," she said sleepily, then yawned.

"Go to sleep. We'll figure out everything in the morning," he whispered. The thought of finding Ashlynn and demanding she tell him what he did wrong came to mind. Looking down at Gwen sleeping peacefully changed his mind. He'd just have to deal with the redheaded female in the morning.

Tonight he was going to sleep beside his mate.

CHAPTER TWENTY-ONE

G wen woke stiff and sore in all the right places. Smiling, she drew in a deep breath and stretched. A dull ache in her muscles was just a reminder of the wonderful lover Markus was. Flinging her arm to the other side of the mattress, she frowned.

Sitting up, she scanned the room. He wasn't there. The bathroom door was open and the light off, so the idea of sneaking into the shower with him was out. *Damn.*

She flung back the sheet and blanket and shivered. The fire had gone out, leaving the room cooler than she remembered when she fell asleep. Then again they hadn't needed the fireplace lit last night, had they?

The smile returned and she eased off the bed and paced to the walk-in closet to dress. Once dressed, she went to the bedroom door and froze. Something was...different.

Annoyed, she marched into the bathroom and flipped on the light. When she faced the mirror, she gasped and placed her hands over her mouth. "Fuck. Oh gods."

A light knock on the door told her it was Elle and she rushed to open it and pull her sister inside the room before anyone else walked by.

Elle's eyes grew round, then she started laughing.

"Elle! It's not funny. I'm glowing."

"I can see that, but why?"

Gwen shook her head and ran back into the bathroom. "I don't know. Last night after Markus and I…" Her gaze darted to Elle when she leaned against the doorframe, "…anyway, after I took his blood. The mating bond snapped in place, but my magic didn't. I wake up and I'm glowing!"

Elle sighed. "I don't think it's anything to freak over. You're not really that bright."

"You're not funny."

"Call your grandmother."

Yes, she could call Aphrodite. Why hadn't Gwen thought of that? Oh yes, she was busy freaking out over her skin. "Aphrodite, I need your assistance."

She hoped that was the correct way to summon the goddess. It wasn't like she'd ever done it before, plus no one had ever told her how. Markus just yelled his father's name, but somehow Gwen knew that wasn't the proper way to call the gods.

A cloud of white and silver smoke formed next to

her, then vanished, leaving Aphrodite in its place. As soon as the goddess saw her, she smiled, wide. "I see he figured out how to unlock your powers."

Gwen held her arms out to her side. "They're not unlocked. My skin is glowing. What did that dragon do to me?"

Aphrodite laughed, grabbed her hand, and tugged her to the door. "Let's go find that dragon and get you outside."

Gwen's stomach churned and her heart started to beat so fast she could feel it in her throat. "Why? What's wrong?"

The goddess stopped and faced her. "Nothing's wrong, dear. You just have a lot of built up energy that needs to be dealt with."

"I don't understand."

"I'll explain. But I only want to do it once."

Gwen nodded and allowed her grandmother to pull her down the stairs and into the living room. Gwen could hear the soft sounds of a piano. Curious, she followed Aphrodite to the baby grand on the other side of the bar.

Aphrodite stopped and motioned for her and Elle to do the same. "I love to listen to him play."

Soothing, classical music filled the room, soft and beautiful. Markus's long fingers gliding over the keys like he was born to play. "I didn't know he played."

"Markus is not used to sharing such things." The

goddess turned to look at her. "You must be patient with him about that characteristic."

Gwen nodded and continued to watch. Suddenly, he slammed down the cover over the keys and stood. Moving too fast for her to track, he was in front of her in less than a second, touching her arms, her face, and starting to lift her shirt.

"Hey. Stop."

He met her gaze, a frown forming and making his forehead wrinkle. "What the hell happened?"

Aphrodite waved off his harsh tone. "The mating is what happened. She needs to release some of this power soon."

Markus scooped her up in his arms and carried her to the back doors, ignoring her protests. Gwen glanced to Elle and scowled. Her best friend tried to keep from falling on the floor in laughter.

Gwen was not amused. She was scared.

Markus set her down in the middle of the backyard and cupped her face so she'd look at him. "There's nothing to be afraid of."

"I don't feel different. Shouldn't I feel…something?"

They looked at Aphrodite. The goddess rolled her eyes. "I don't know. Okay. Gwen, do you feel anything that wasn't there yesterday?"

Gwen thought about it. "Markus. I feel him and the bond and his dragon."

Aphrodite nodded. "Of course. It's Markus."

Gwen scoffed at the goddess's "simple" answer. "What is Markus? Please, Grandma, just tell me."

The goddess blinked, then her eyes watered. Shit, what had Gwen said to upset her? She was about to apologize when Aphrodite pulled her into a tight hug. "I've waited for so long to be able to hear you call me that."

Gwen relaxed in her arms. "I'm sorry for blaming you."

Aphrodite pulled back and wiped under her eyes. "Don't be, dear. Okay. You are glowing because your body and mind don't know what to do with the excess power running through you. It's not able to get through the mating bond with Markus or exit another way, so it just builds and you start to glow."

Gwen stared, not really knowing what else to do. "Make it stop."

Aphrodite turned around as if searching for something or someone. Then she dropped her shoulders and walked back to the back door. Gwen looked at the doorway and saw Elle standing in the shaded area of the porch. When the goddess approached Elle, she conjured a white cloak and handed it to Elle.

Smiling, Elle put it on. The garment covered her whole body. The two of them came back over to Gwen and Markus and Elle said, "This is great. Can I keep it?"

Aphrodite nodded. "Of course." Turning back to Gwen, she said, "Now I want you to stand with your feet slightly apart and your arms straight out to your sides, palms down. Everyone else move back a few steps."

Gwen did as she was instructed. Her skin warmed, almost like she was running a fever. Then a burst of energy shot through her, making her feel jittery. It was like the time she drank a pot of coffee during finals in college, only worse. She didn't know how much longer she'd be able to stand there.

Aphrodite stepped into her line of sight. "Gwen, look at me and breathe."

Gwen met her gaze. "I feel like I need to go for a run."

"It's the built up power. Okay, focus inward and find the source of your powers. You'll know when you find it. It'll be a white, bright ball of energy. It usually gathers in your chest area."

Gwen nodded and closed her eyes. Using what she'd learned from years of yoga, she entered a meditative state and searched for the inner light. It didn't take her long to find the source of her "inner glow."

"Found it," she said.

Aphrodite spoke softly. "Try to push that energy out to your hands and feet and allow it flow into the earth."

Gwen willed the light to move to her hands and feet, then pushed it out, into the earth. When she was done, she took a deep, cleansing breath, drawing in the salty ocean air. She opened her eyes and met her grandmother's gaze. "I feel so much better."

Aphrodite smiled and took her hands in hers.

Markus stepped up behind her, amazing her on how sensitive she'd become to his presence. Leaning back against his warm chest, she sighed. His warmth surrounded her, soothing and erotic.

Markus placed his arms on her shoulders and kissed her head before speaking. "Why did it take so long for her powers to surface?"

The goddess dropped her shoulders and let go of Gwen's hands. "Her powers were never locked, not really."

A growl rumbled in Markus's chest, vibrating Gwen's back. "Explain, goddess."

Aphrodite glared at him sharply. "Don't get that growly tone with me. Because she is half goddess of fate, I can't bind her powers. The Fates are off Zeus's radar for the most part, and they never spoke of Alexia's fall to earth to be with a demi-god."

Markus growled again. "Would he know that Gwen's mother was a goddess?"

Aphrodite shook her head. "Zeus never paid close attention to the descendants. That's what you and your brothers are here for."

His irritation shot through the mate bond, shocking Gwen. She reached up and squeezed his hands. "So why haven't I felt my powers before now?"

The goddess shrugged. "I'm not sure. It could be the protective spell I cast over you when you were born. Your father could have tried to bind your powers." She paused to walk toward the gardens as if in thought.

Gwen wiggled out of Markus's arms and followed her. When they reached the roses, Aphrodite turned. "The powers you would have inherited from me aren't the type you feel like most of the other gods. Mine come from the heart and from what's inside. As for the Fates, it's in the words and the will. So you've had the power all along, you just didn't know how to use it."

Now Gwen was growing impatient. She had three days to learn how to kick ass, magic style, and her grandmother wasn't being very helpful. "So how do I use these powers I never knew I had?"

Aphrodite glanced at her over her shoulder and smiled. "You must trust in yourself and open your mind to all possibilities. Your greatest power is your will to survive and protect those you love."

Without another word, Aphrodite dematerialized. Gwen gaped at the empty space in front her, then turned to Markus. "That is so annoying."

Laughing, he grabbed her arm and tugged her to him. "Believe me, I know."

CHAPTER TWENTY-TWO

Gwen formed an energy ball between her hands, lifted her lashes to focus on her target and, with a smirk, threw it. A flash of bright, white light went off as the god bolt nailed its target. Seth roared and his dragon flashed in his eyes right before he dropped to his knees.

"Damn, female. That fucking hurts."

Markus laughed from where he leaned against the wall. "You volunteered. Suck it up."

Seth rose to feet, holding his hands up in surrender. "That was two days ago when she was learning to control her powers. The hits of energies didn't hurt then."

Gwen folded her arms over her chest and cocked a brow. "Do you want to go another round on the mats?"

Seth shook his head. "Nope. I've been embarrassed

enough for the century." Glancing over to Markus, he added, "I thinks it's time for Ash to make that call."

Markus growled, but Gwen could feel the dragon's pride and acceptance of the strength she gained over the last two days. The man might not want her to face Garrick, but she needed to face the monster that killed her parents.

And she was ready.

Markus pushed off the wall and prowled toward her, heat in his stare. When he was inches from her, he scooped her up and walked to the door. "Seth, tell Ash to make the call and that she'll meet him tomorrow afternoon."

Gwen meet his gaze. "Why the afternoon?"

"Because if she tells him to meet her at night, he'd know we set her up to it."

"What if he suspects anyway?"

A wicked and cool smile appeared. "That's why Ty and I will be there."

Gwen's heart dropped. "What? He'll sense you as soon as you get too close."

"He'll sense me on you and know we're bound together the moment you are in the same room. He'll expect us to crash his party."

Not liking his plan, she wiggled until he lowered her to her feet. Crossing her arms, she glared at him. "You need to work on your communication skills. What do you have planned?"

That lazy smile that annoyed her and turned her on at the same time lifted his lips. "We plan to be close enough to get you out of there, but we will attack if it is necessary."

Gwen studied him for a moment. She shouldn't be surprised that he'd follow them. Damn stubborn man. A part of her was happy to have the backup, because she was scared out of her mind about that mission. Yet, she couldn't back out. She needed to try to bring Garrick down a few notches.

She was about to turn away from him to head to the study where Ash was going to make the call when a thought came to mind. "Shouldn't I have the ability to teleport? I mean with my powers unlocked, I should be able to, right?"

Markus's dark brows dipped as if considering the question. "Yes, I believe so."

"Why haven't you showed me how?"

"Because it'd take longer than three days for you to master it. Teleporting takes concentration and a great deal of focus. We can't teleport to just anywhere. It has to be a place you've been before and it takes a lot of energy to do so."

"I'm stronger now. It's important that I at least know how to do it. Plus you could help me in case something went wrong and I *needed* to teleport out of there."

Satisfaction sparked inside her at the narrow-eyed expression Markus gave her. Ha, she bet he hadn't thought about that, she was sure. Lifting her brows at him and waiting for a response, he let out a low, irritated growl. "Fine. Close your eyes and visualize the inside of my study."

Obeying, she brought up the image of his study, the furniture, bookcases, and even the security cameras mounted in the corners of the room. "Okay, now what?"

"Imagine that you are standing inside the room and wish it so."

She imagined herself standing in the middle of the room. Focusing on being in the study, she silently wished she was there. Nothing happened, so she opened her eyes. "What did I do wrong?"

He smiled as if he'd known she wouldn't be able to do it. "You have to desire it with all your will."

Now he told her. Closing her eyes again, she repeated the act, but this time she put her heart into it like her life depended on it. A moment later she felt a pull, then she was surrounded by darkness and the feeling of being dragged through a thick watery substance very fast. The next instant light flashed and she was standing in the study.

Gwen started laughing as she turned around to see everyone in the room. Ash sat on the sofa with a cell phone in hand. Elle sat in an armchair to her right, smiling. Ty, Seth, Zavier and Drake stood close by, staring at Gwen in disbelief. Markus materialized beside her a moment later.

Looking at him, Gwen said, "That was great."

Markus grunted and reached out to touch her cheek. "How are you feeling?"

"I feel good. A little dizzy, but good."

He shook his head and she saw a slight smile form before he turned to his brothers. "That was her first time, so no one get any ideas of encouraging her do it during the mission."

Gwen frowned and pinched his arm, making him jerk and glare down at her. "I will if my life is in danger."

He lowered his head so they were nose-to-nose. "That would be the *only* time you try."

Rolling her eyes, she walked over to the sofa and sat between Elle and Ash. Both women tried to hide their smiles, which did nothing to help Gwen appear mad at her dragon.

I'll deal with you later. In my bed.

Gwen met Markus's gaze as he spoke those words telepathically. Heat spread through her like wildfire. Biting her lower lip, she thought back to him, *I look forward to it.*

His eyes flashed light blue, but it was gone before the others took notice. "Ashlynn, make the call."

Everyone fell silent as Ash dialed and pressed the phone to her ear. Sitting as close to Ash as she was, and the fact that her hearing was as good as her dragon mate's, Gwen heard when Garrick answered the phone.

"Well, to what do I owe this honor?"

Ash rolled her eyes. "I hope you're happy for ruining my plan."

He growled. "I did no such thing. As far as I know, you've betrayed me and moved in with my brothers."

Ash ignored his statement. "I told you I'd get that female for you and that's what I was doing."

Garrick paused briefly before speaking. "What was I supposed to think when you killed four of my best scouts? Then I track you down at the dragon's mansion. I can't read your mind."

Ash glanced at Gwen then Markus. "I figured you trusted your best hunter to do what was needed to bring back Gwen."

"What about the other female? I want both of them."

"Danielle isn't with your brothers."

Another growl sound from the phone that made Gwen's skin prickle. "Where is she?"

Ash fisted her hand in her lap as if trying to rein in some control. "I don't know. She wasn't at the castle when I got there. They must have hidden her."

"Find out where."

"She's fourth generation and no use to us."

"No, Tom was sure she was a first generation descendant."

Gwen stiffened at the mention of her father's name and locked gazes with Markus. Slowly, he shook his head, reminding her to stay quiet. Ash reached over and took her hand. Shocked at the friendly contact, Gwen gently squeezed, then reach over and linked her fingers with Elle.

Ash let out a dramatic sigh. "Danielle is useless to us," she repeated, then added, "I have a very reliable resource. Gwen is the one we need."

There was a long silence before he spoke again. "Bring the female to me now. You know where. Don't disappoint me."

He hung up and Ash did the same, then dropped her head back on the sofa. "It's done. There was still a lot of suspicion in his tone, though."

Markus grinned. "Let him be. He makes mistakes when he's on edge."

GWEN ZIPPED and unzipped her jacket nervously as she waited for Ash to meet her in the foyer. She'd spent the last three days training, building her physical and magical strengths. It paid off big time. Both she and Markus were surprised at how fast she'd learned to balance her power after she and her dragon completed the mating bond.

Just the thought of the mating ritual, along with every night since, made her skin tighten and grow warm.

Awareness rose inside her, hot and erotic. Whirling around, she smiled at the sight of Markus in all black. Damn, he looked good enough to lick.

Ty stepped up next to him dressed the same way. Gwen saw one dark brow rise over the shades Ty never took off.

Ash walked in from the great room, shaking her head as she studied the men. "Are we robbing a bank along the way?"

Ty took a step, but Markus stopped him by slamming a palm against his chest. "You two can duke it out later, but now we have to go fuck up Gary's day."

Gwen giggled, and Markus glared at her. Waving him off, she said, "I'm fine. But you said Gary. It sounded funny coming from you."

Ash touched her forearm. Gwen met the other woman's gaze, she saw the humor there along with sorrow and dread. Sobering, Gwen nodded and covered Ash's hand. "I understand that you must do whatever you have to."

Ash extracted her hand and walked out the front door.

Markus stepped up beside Gwen and laced his fingers with hers. "You need to be careful. Keep an eye out for every possibility."

"I will. It's Ash that I'm worried about."

"What do you mean?"

Gwen raised one shoulder. "I don't know. Maybe I'm just too wired."

Taking a deep breath, she released Markus's hand and followed Ash out of the house. Outside she spotted Ash at the edge of the cliff, staring over it. "Ash?"

She turned to face her and gave a short nod. Together they followed the narrow path down the mountain toward the beach. The pickup location was a small rundown beach house several miles west of Serenity Cove, but they never made it that far. Imperials materialized in front of them.

Show time, Gwen said telepathically to Markus somewhere nearby, but she couldn't see him.

Ash spoke to a black haired man, the apparent leader of this group. "It's about damn time. I thought I'd have to go to the beach house and call Garrick."

The man narrowed his eyes for a brief moment before he motioned to a man on his left and grabbed Ash's upper arm at the same time. Gwen spared a look at Ash, sure this wasn't part of the plan, but used the surprise to her advantage. "I can't believe you set me up!"

Ash tried to jerk away from the descendant. "What are you doing, idiot? I was bringing the love goddess in."

"We have our orders."

Then the men teleported away with them. A moment later Gwen and Ash were thrown in separate cells. Fear flared to life, consuming her. Markus couldn't follow them if they'd been teleported. Or could he?

Shit. This was bad.

Think, Gwen.

Panic started to make its ugly appearance and her

chest tightened. *Breathe and think*. She would not have a panic attack. *Damn it.*

"Gwen."

Hearing her name, she turned and met Ash's pissed off glare. "How do we get out of here?"

Ash's green eyes darkened, her lips pursed as she held up a fisted hand to show Gwen the thick metal cuff around her wrist. "This dampens my powers. Bastard thinks he's so smart." She smiled, cruel and vindictive.

Gwen shivered, glad that Ash was on her side. The Imperials didn't put a cuff on her. That told her they didn't know her powers were unlocked and couldn't sense them. Then again, Aphrodite said Gwen's powers were never fully bound.

Meeting Ash's gaze again, Gwen studied her. Ash appeared more like the goddess she was than she did before. Gwen wondered just how powerful she was. "You have a plan, right?"

Ash nodded once. "The cells are rigged to alert Garrick once they are open. So we wait for his royal ass to come and gloat over his capture."

Gwen's stomach soured. Ash's words were filled with so much venom that Gwen had to suppress another shiver. Footsteps sounded from her right, making her blood freeze in her veins.

Garrick came into view and memories of that horrific night slammed into her, bringing the pain and built up anger to the fore. He stopped outside her cell, an evil grin spread across his lips. Leaning into the bars, he inhaled deeply and his grin turned into a wide smile. "I see Markus wasted no time to claim you as his own. So tell me, did he take you by force?"

Gwen jerked back, fury fueling her power. "I bet Hades has a special place in Tartarus reserved just for you."

His eyes went pitch black then the pupil lengthened, transforming into dragon's eyes. A week ago, she'd have crumbled into a panting mess on the floor as fear overrode her ability to think and breathe. *But not today.*

Her anxiety wouldn't control her. Not anymore. Hell, she'd spent the last three days sparring with Markus and Seth. And Drake, who had surprised her in the kitchen, growled at her, and shifted his eyes from human to dragon. When she held up a hand with a soft-ball size energy ball in it instead of running, he gave her the first smile she'd seen from him and left the room.

If Drake failed to scare her, she wouldn't let Garrick do it either.

"I see the goddess has a backbone after all." Garrick reached for her through the bars. Gwen stepped back, out of his reach.

Ash made a noise like a cross between a growl and a hiss. "I wouldn't touch her bare skin. She's already cursed one of the dragons."

Gwen jerked her gaze to the other woman and narrowed her eyes. She saw Ash's lie as plain as if it were written across her forehead. Gwen wanted to smile and thank her, but she had to keep up the false sense of betrayal toward her new friend. "Shut up! I can't believe I trusted you."

Ash shrugged and turned to sit on a bench in the corner of her cell. "You were so easy to lure away from your dragon mate, I couldn't pass it up."

Garrick laughed, but there was no humor in it. "I'll deal with you later, Ashlynn. For now I need something from Aphrodite's granddaughter."

Reaching for her again, he growled when she darted to the other side of the small cell. Her heart pounded hard against her ribs. With a growl, Garrick conjured a hypodermic needle with some kind of bluish tinted liquid inside it. She swallowed hard and pressed her back to the stone wall at the back of the cell.

Ash came to her feet and rattled the bars. "Garrick. You can't inject her with that."

Gwen glanced to Ash and her heart sank as she saw real fear in the goddess's gaze. "What is that?"

"It's the serum he uses to unlock the descendants' powers, but it also has a binding agent in it that would bind your will to his."

Fuck.

Gwen started to shake all over. Her lungs felt tight, making her take short, deep breaths. *Markus, if you can hear me you need to hurry the fuck up and get here.*

Gods, she hoped he was able to track her because she and Ash needed a large diversion.

The lock on the cell clicked, and Gwen jumped. Fear sped up her heart rate as she stared at the needle as

Garrick slid the door open and stepped inside. Her stomach churned and she was sure she was going to be sick if he touched her.

When he lunged for her, she'd already begun the process of teleportation. She flashed to the outside of the cell and slammed the door into place, clicking the lock and palming the key the idiot left behind.

Garrick roared and slammed into the bars. Gwen let out a squeak and rushed over to Ash's cell and unlocked it. By the time she stepped out, Garrick had shifted into a very large and scary as all Hades black dragon. The cell no longer contained him. By the size of him, neither would the room they were in.

Ash grabbed her hand and tugged her through the room that Gwen could now tell was some kind of lab and computer center. "Wait!"

Gwen pulled her hand free from Ash's and rushed to a desk with a laptop and several files and devices on it. Ash was at her side in a flash, picking up objects and stuffing them inside a backpack. Gwen didn't know where the woman got the bag, but she really didn't care. She was relieved for her quick thinking.

Ash shoved the bag at her and the building they were in shook, large pieces of the ceiling raining around them.

"The place is going to cave in. Take this and run." Ash pointed to an exit behind Gwen.

Shaking her head, Gwen said, "Not without you."

"You have to. Don't worry about me. Now go."

Before Gwen realized what Ash had done, she was being pulled through time and space and materialized outside the building seconds before it collapsed into a pile of stone and dust.

"Ash!" Gwen fell to her knees with the backpack pressed to her chest, tears streaming down her face.

CHAPTER TWENTY-THREE

Markus landed in a large field about fifteen miles west of Serenity Cove, folded his wings into his back and shifted to his human form. Scanning the area, he couldn't see anything for miles. A growl rumbled through his chest and he fisted his hands.

Where the fuck was Gwen?

Ty landed beside him and remained in dragon form. His red and gold scales shimmered in the setting sunlight. He blew out a breath through his noise, drawing Markus's attention. *I don't smell either of the females.*

"Me either." Markus was beyond the point of rational thought. His mate was missing and it was his fault for allowing her to go on the mission.

As soon as the thought formed, he regretted it. She wasn't a prisoner and he couldn't keep her from doing anything. If he told her no, she'd have gone in anyway.

"I'm going to try to track her through the mating bond again."

Ty turned in the opposite direction, giving Markus room to search for the connection to his mate. Apparently, they had to be within a certain proximity in order to connect. The lack of connection was driving his dragon insane.

Ash was right. Dragons did go insane when they lost a mate. He didn't doubt that the human was dragged under with the beast.

Taking a deep breath, he closed his eyes, and sent out his senses, searching out as far as he could. On his second pass of the area, he felt it. *Gwen's pain.* Not physical, but emotional.

"I got them," Markus shouted and took off in a run toward the west.

Overhead, Ty followed about twenty feet off the ground. *There's a group of trees and a building ten yards ahead. Dude, the building looks like it collapsed or something. I'm going ahead to take a closer look.*

Dread cut through his heart and all he could think about was Gwen trapped inside the ruins of a building. He knew she wasn't dead because of their bond, but he couldn't tell if she was hurt due to the amount of emotions flooding the link between them as he got closer.

Finally, he reached the grouping of trees and pushed his legs faster. When he saw the torn down building, he skidded to a stop, chest rising and falling as his heart pounded in his head. Ty squatted down next to Gwen, his hand out. Shaking her head, she cried into her hands.

Markus walked over and lifted her into his arms, cradling her to his chest.

Instantly, her arms wrapped around him. "Ash didn't make it. She wouldn't leave with me."

"Shh." He spared a look at Ty, who was now standing, glaring at the ruins with murder in his gaze. "Ty, let's go, man. She's immortal, remember."

Without a word, his brother turned, ran, and shifted into his dragon. Markus let Ty go, because if his guess was right, then Ash was Ty's mate. He needed the time it took to fly home to clear his head.

Markus spotted a backpack on the ground where Gwen had dropped it and picked it up before teleporting them to the mansion. Markus carried Gwen through the front door and straight to his study while sending out a telepathic message to his brothers to meet him there. Setting her on the sofa, he positioned the pillow that she threw at him a couple of nights before under her head.

Tears filled her sky blue eyes as she stared at him. "We have to search the ruins for her. I have to know…"

Brushing a strand of hair from her face, he said, "Ash is immortal. A building collapsing would not kill her."

She held his gaze for several moments as if she was trying to let it all soak in. Finally she nodded. "She teleported me out right before the building collapsed."

"Why did it fall in?"

"Garrick." A shiver passed through her before she continued. "He tried to inject me with some serum. Ash panicked and told him not to. Ash said it had a binding agent in it. When he opened my cell and came inside with me, I teleported outside and closed him in."

"That's good. What's in the backpack?"

Glancing to the bag in his hand, she smiled a little. "Ash stuffed things in there. I'm not sure what's all in there."

Zavier, Drake, Seth, and Elle entered the study. Elle rushed over to Gwen. Markus stepped aside to allow the females some time while he took Zavier the bag. "See what you can get from the contents of this."

Z opened the bag and a wide grin spread across his face. "This is nice. There's a laptop, files, jump drives, disks. Oh man, I'm in techno-heaven."

Markus shook his head and glanced back at Gwen. His heart ached from the lack of contact with her. He needed to get her alone, soon, to make sure she was truly okay.

Turning back to his brothers, he filled them in on what happened to the building, Ash, and Gwen. "Ty didn't take the fact that Ash didn't make it out of the building well. I don't expect him back anytime soon."

Zavier and Drake nodded. Seth cursed low. "The sorry ass stubborn male will be searching for her."

Markus agreed. They'd all noticed how much the female got under Ty's skin. He couldn't seem to leave her alone, always watching and waiting. For what,

Markus had no clue. His only guess was they were mates and both denied it.

The air around them shifted from calm to electric, then Ares materialized next to him. "War," Markus muttered, really not wanting to talk with the god at the moment.

Ares rolled his eyes. "I only came to tell you that Garrick is wounded, badly, but he is still alive."

Markus jerked his gaze to his father. "Aren't we feeling like sharing for once? Why are you telling us this?"

Ares stepped closer to him, coming nose-to-nose with him. "Because when he heals, he's going to want revenge on every one of you, including Ashlynn."

Markus raised a brow. "The female lives?"

Ares backed off to move around the room. "I'm not at liberty to say."

Markus took that as a yes and as the gods were using the redhead minor goddess more than as a spy. She had another reason for being there and they weren't finished with her.

Too tired to think and needing to feel his mate under him, Markus stalked toward Gwen. He held out his hand, she smiled, and took it. Tugging her to her feet, he glance at Elle. "Do you mind if I steal your sister for the next twenty-four hours or so?"

Elle shook her head. "No. You two need time together." Standing, she kissed him on the cheek.

"Thank you for making sure she came back home." Then she left the room.

Gwen cupped his face and kissed him. He wrapped his arms around her and teleported them to his...no, *their* room. Smiling, he laid her down on the bed. "I know what it is to love someone so much that it hurts to be without them."

Surprise lit up her eyes. "Do you?"

He nodded. "I love you. I can't ever let you do anything like you did today again. It drove my dragon and I insane to think of the ways I could have lost you."

It came out more demanding then he intended, but she didn't flinch or draw away from him. Her eyes began to water as she held his gaze and said, "I love you, too. And I don't plan on doing anything like that again. Just promise me one thing."

"What?"

"If the day ever comes that you do capture Garrick, I want to be there to see him go down."

Markus's smile widened and his heart warmed. "Deal."

Taking his face in her hands, she pulled him to her. Nipping at his lower lip, she said, "Make love to me and make me forget about your evil brother."

His dragon growled in approval inside his head. Dipping his head, he bit her lower lip and tugged. "Anything for my mate."

EPILOGUE

Ash lay on her mother's bed, wishing the goddess would hurry. She ached everywhere, not to mention it hurt like fuck to breathe. Her ribs and lungs took the worst of it. In her concern for getting Gwen out of the building and away from Garrick, Ash had failed to hear him approach from behind until the dagger jammed into her back, puncturing a lung. She broke a couple of ribs when the bastard knocked her across the room.

Then the building caved in.

Artemis eased down on the bed and smoothed her hair from her face. "No one can ever know I rescued you."

"Of course, Mother."

The goddess opened an amber-colored jar and dipped out a creamy salve, then spread it over her ribs.

"The terms for your mission were that I not interfere, no matter what."

Ash sighed and lifted her hand weakly. "I know, Mother. That was why I didn't summon you."

"And what would you have done if I hadn't shown up?" Artemis met her stare and frowned.

"Survived. After I passed out and healed myself."

Her mother rolled her eyes and replaced the cap on the jar. "Garrick is injured." A smile lifted her lips. "You almost killed him with the god bolt you threw at him. It hit his heart, you know."

Ash smiled and would have laughed if it didn't hurt so much. She never got the chance to hit Garrick with her power, but she understood what her mother was saying. Artemis had hit Garrick and most likely made him think it was Ash.

"What about the mission?" Ash asked.

"You will stay here and heal then go back to your dragon and pass judgment."

Dread rippled through her. Ash hadn't even come close to completing her true mission. If she failed at proving Ty's innocence it would kill what humanity was left inside her to bring him in to be sentenced to death by the gods.

However, she was a servant of the gods and would do her job.

"Yes, Mother. I won't let you down."

$\sim$

The End

To stay up to date with current and new releases, sign up
for her newsletter

Next in the Dragons of Ares world:
Ashes of War

ABOUT LIA DAVIS

Lia Davis is the USA Today bestselling author of more than sixty books, including her fan favorite Ashwood Falls Series.

A lifelong fan of magic, mystery, romance and adventure, Lia's novels feature compassionate alpha heroes and strong leading ladies, plenty of heat, and happily-ever-afters.

Lia makes her home in Northeast Florida where she battles hurricanes and humidity like one of her heroines.

When she's not writing, she loves to spend time with her family, travel, read, enjoy nature, and spoil her kitties.

She also loves to hear from her readers. Send her a note at lia@authorliadavis.com!

Follow Lia on Social Media

Website: http://www.authorliadavis.com/
Newsletter: http://www.
subscribepage.com/authorliadavis.newsletter

Facebook author fan page: https://www.facebook.com/novelsbylia/
Facebook Fan Club: https://www.facebook.com/groups/LiaDavisFanClub/
Twitter: https://twitter.com/novelsbylia
Instagram: https://www.instagram.com/authorliadavis/
BookBub: https://www.bookbub.com/authors/lia-davis
Pinterest: http://www.pinterest.com/liadavis35/
Goodreads: http://www.goodreads.com/author/show/5829989.Lia_Davis

Their Royal Ash

Tempting the Wolf

Hexed with Sass (part of the Milly Taiden Sassy Ever After World)

Claiming Her Dragons (Part of the Milly Taiden Paranormal Dating Agency)

Contemporaries

Pleasures of the Heart Series

Single Titles

His Guarded Heart (MM)